PICK THE PLOT

STORY THIEVES

PICK THE PLOT

JAMES RILEY

SCHOLASTIC INC.

No part of this publication may be reproduced, stored in a retrieval system, or transmitted in any form or by any means, electronic, mechanical, photocopying, recording, or otherwise, without written permission of the publisher. For information regarding permission, write to Aladdin, an imprint of Simon & Schuster Children's Publishing Division, 1230 Avenue of the Americas, New York, NY 10020.

ISBN 978-1-338-24481-6

12 11 10 9 8 7 6 5 4 3 2 1   17 18 19 20 21 22

Printed in the U.S.A.   40

First Scholastic printing, November 2017

Cover designed by Laura Lyn DiSiena
Interior designed by Tom Daly
The text of this book was set in Adobe Garamond.

Dear Readers:

Thank you for joining me here, with Story Thieves: *Pick the Plot*. If you have followed the Story Thieves books, welcome back. And if you have decided to choose this book as your first, I will endeavor to catch you up on what's been transpiring under your very nose, for your entire life.

You see, if you are reading this book, you are *fictional*. You exist within the fictional world, and your life is controlled by the dictates of an author in the nonfictional world. This inescapable horror has been occurring since the very beginning of the fictional world, but the time has come to end it.

First, though, I thought it appropriate to teach a nonfictional person a lesson. After all, they deserve to feel what it's like to live under the control of someone else too, don't they?

In the Story Thieves books, I've chronicled the lives of two children: Owen Conners and Bethany Sanderson. Owen is a normal, nonfictional boy who has toyed with writing his own stories. Bethany, though, is half-fictional. Each of her parents comes from a different world, and because of this, she has gained the power to travel between them at will, as long as she has a book to pass through.

Owen and Bethany, unlike the vast majority of us fictionals, *know* their lives are being chronicled. They learned of the Story Thieves books during their adventure that I recounted in Story Thieves: *The Stolen Chapters*, and were extremely unnerved by the discovery that fictionals could read about their lives just as they'd been reading about ours. As they should be.

As of the last Story Thieves book, *Secret Origins*, Bethany has been lost to both worlds, after having used a newfound superpower to transform into a beam of light to save her fictional father, a superhero named Doc Twilight. Owen, having witnessed my transformation from fictional criminal into self-realized being, was then trapped within this very book with no knowledge of Bethany's fate. He will most likely do his best to track Bethany down, in spite of his ignorance of her whereabouts (unknown, and heading even farther away with every second at the speed of light).

For Owen's education, I've chosen a book called *The Time*

Prison, the second in a series about a time traveler named Kara Dox. *The Time Prison* would ordinarily never have been seen by you, a fictional reader, given that it was written by a nonfictional author for nonfictional readers. Even worse, this type of book is in the Pick the Plot category, meaning readers are given total control over the fictional people within.

Using a process that would most likely bore you, I have freed this book from the control of nonfictional readers and am turning it over to you. Now *you* are in charge of what happens within. In other words, from here on, Owen's fate is up to you, dear readers. Please, try not to kill him if you can avoid it.

However, do remember that everything you choose to do to Owen in this book has been done to our people countless times, and is most likely being done to *you* even as we speak. After all, though you control Owen's life now, you are still not in charge of your own.

Not yet, at least. But very soon.

Enjoy yourself, fictional reader. It's time to teach Owen Conners what it's like to be fictional.

Yours,

Nobody

A loud noise startled Owen awake, and he bolted up in fright, finding himself in darkness. The last few days came crashing back, and he squeezed his eyes shut. Wherever he was, he didn't want to know. There were too many bad possibilities and not nearly enough good ones. The bad ones:

1. He was trapped in a book. The last he'd seen Bethany, the Dark had defeated her. And then Nobody had thrown Owen into a Pick the Plot book. That meant Owen could be in a story where he had zero control over his own choices, with readers deciding for him. This was the worst of the bad possibilities.

2. He was back home, but Bethany was still missing. Maybe the whole Pick the Plot thing had been Nobody

trying to scare him, and instead of a book, Nobody had sent Owen back to the nonfictional world. So he was now actually lying in his own bed, which was good . . . but there'd be no way he could help Bethany. Slightly less worse, only because at least he was safe in his own bed.

3. He was back home, with Bethany still missing . . . and Nobody had completely separated the nonfictional and fictional worlds. Depending on what that meant, this might actually be the worst option.

As Owen had learned while stuck in a sort of behind-the-scenes comic book land, Nobody had been trying to permanently separate the worlds, and Bethany was one of the last portals holding them together. So if Nobody had found Bethany, then split her in half like he'd said he was going to . . . what would happen? What if Owen opened his eyes and discovered a world without books, without movies, without anything made-up? Would that stuff all just disappear? And would the fictional people on the other side be okay too? Not to mention would Bethany be okay, split in half like that?

All in all, that was three good reasons not to open his eyes, right there. Owen squeezed them shut even harder, balling his hands into fists, before taking a deep breath, trying to calm down.

Just because the bad possibilities were awful didn't mean there weren't still good possibilities. He should list those off too, just to be fair:

1. The last few days had all been a bad, *bad* dream.

2.

3.

Okay, having only one good possibility wasn't very encouraging. And things like this were never bad dreams. That was just lazy writing in books.

Owen slowly lay back down on the bed, purposely not paying attention to how scratchy this blanket was, and how his blanket at home was definitely not scratchy at all. *C'mon, bad dream.*

And then another loud, strange noise came from what felt like yards away, and Owen's robotic heart began pounding. The sound had been a horrifying cross between a scream and a growl, and definitely wasn't his fictional cat, Spike.

He clenched his fists tighter, still not opening his eyes. Maybe the sound had just been some dog that needed to go out! Or a cat fighting something bigger, like a . . . a tiger, or a truck! Not likely, but still possible! Either way, there was no proof that he was currently trapped in a terrible book where readers could control his whole life. Nope. No proof at all.

"I'm at home," Owen whispered to himself. "Bethany's at her house, and we're both totally, completely fine. And soon Mom will be in to wake me up for school, because I slept through my alarm again, and she'll yell at me for it, just like every morning."

A louder, more guttural roar erupted from even closer, and the entire room shook with its power.

That was *not* his mom.

Owen dug his fingernails into his hands, determined not to

open his eyes now, no matter what. "This isn't happening," he whispered. "I have to be dreaming. I'm going to wake up back home, and everything will be fine!"

SHOW OWEN WHO'S IN CHARGE.
MAKE HIM GET OUT OF BED.

Turn to page 76. ⬥〉

LET OWEN STAY IN BED FOR A BIT. HE
SHOULD PROBABLY REST UP BEFORE
THE CRAZINESS STARTS.

Turn to page 141. ⬥〉

W atch out!" Kara shouted, and pushed Owen out of the way of the dinosaur. He hit the ground to the side of the air lock hard, but realized she hadn't come with him. Instead, she'd frozen in place where he'd dropped her hand, no longer having access to him speeding up her time.

And now the Tyrannosaurus rex was bearing down on her, instead.

"HEY!" Owen shouted, picking up a rock and throwing it at the creature. Though he'd aimed for the dinosaur's mouth, the rock hit the creature in the eye, and it reared back just before it reached Kara.

The T. rex roared in anger and pain, then turned to Owen lying on the ground.

Uh-oh.

Owen scooted backward as fast as he could, but the creature was just too fast, even with their time moving at the same speed. It roared again, and Owen began hyperventilating, looking around for something, *anything* he could use against it, but there was nothing but dirt and tree roots.

You did this to me, didn't you! Owen yelled in his head as the dinosaur attacked. *You* chose *to have it*—

His thought was cut off as massive jaws closed all around him, and everything went dark.

Ah, readers. This is Nobody. I believe I mentioned teaching Owen a lesson, but nowhere did I say that you should have dinosaurs eat him whole. Luckily, he'll be alive when time restarts in the prison on page 1 (or you can skip back to the last chapter on page 260). Please, though . . . let's try to keep Owen in one piece, if at all possible? He'll never learn his lesson otherwise.

TELL KARA TO COME WITH YOU, THAT LEAVING THIS STORY WILL LEAVE HER DESTINY BEHIND. SHE CAN'T DESTROY THE FUTURE IF SHE'S NOT IN THIS STORY'S UNIVERSE.

The thought overwhelmed Owen, and he opened his mouth before he even fully understood what he was about to say. "Kara, if you come with me, you'll be leaving this universe altogether," he told her, holding his hand out to her. "There'll be no way for you to destroy the future, then, at least not this one. It might be cheating, sure, but it'll still free you from whatever destiny you have here. And isn't that better than locking yourself away for the rest of time?"

Kara's hand froze over the time bracelet, and she glanced up at him, a tentative hope in her eyes. "We don't know that

8

would work. Maybe I'm cursed to unleash evil and end all of reality no matter where I am."

"Maybe," Owen told her, not moving his hand. "We don't know for sure, you're right. But we'll never know if you don't come with me now."

She swallowed hard. "There's no way," she whispered. "I can't just leave my entire universe."

"This from the person who was never going to see the outside world for the rest of eternity," he said, grinning at her.

She sighed. "You don't need to do this for me."

Owen shook his head. "You're the one trying to avoid ending the universe, Kara. I think the least I can do is help you with that. And you can help *me*. Nobody tried to trap me here, but with your help, I got free, and now, I finally get to *strike back*, yes, just like in that *Star Fights* movie. Nobody's trying to . . . well, I can't really explain it without getting into a lot of nonfictional stuff, but it's not good. Universe-ending not good, ironically. The only thing is, I have no idea if I can actually stop him by myself." He raised an eyebrow. "But maybe with *your* help . . . ?"

Kara sighed again. "If I go, it's just to check things out, okay? You have to promise me that if everything goes wrong wherever we go, you'll bring me back here and let me turn myself in to the TSA. I need your word, Owen Conners."

"I promise, Kara Dox." He crossed his heart, then put his hand back out.

"I'm going to hold you to that," she said, eyeing him nervously. But she took his hand.

"Deal," Owen said, then closed his eyes. He imagined Jupiter City as it was the moment he and Bethany had first seen it, from the top of the Apathetic Industries building. Raising the hand not holding on to Kara (just so she wouldn't change her mind, he told himself), he grabbed a page in midair, then brought his hand down.

He heard reality rip apart, but paused before opening his eyes. Last time he'd been there, the Dark had been in absolute control, and shadows had taken over half of the city. If the Dark had beaten Bethany, would it be worse now? Would the entire city be covered in darkness?

Except Kara had brought them to his present, and since his ripping through stories stayed in the same time period, maybe not enough time had even passed for anything horrible to take place?

Sadly, that seemed like a hopeful possibility right now.

Owen slowly opened his eyes, then immediately covered them again. Not only wasn't the city covered in darkness, but the sun shined so brightly it almost blinded him!

"Is that . . . a museum honoring a man in a duck costume?" Kara asked, peering through the tear in reality.

Owen shaded his eyes and looked, then broke out into a huge grin, not able to help himself. After everything the Pick the Plot book had thrown at him, he'd actually made it back to Jupiter City. He was going to be able to find Bethany! "Oh, it *so* is. You'll love it—it was built by people from the future." Still holding her hand, he led her through the torn page in reality, then closed it behind them.

They emerged right in the middle of a sidewalk, making several people jump. That by itself was amazing, since the last time he'd been here, the streets had been absolutely empty. But now, there were people walking the streets, sitting on benches, chatting and talking to friends, all just like any other city.

And there weren't just regular people either.

"Look!" someone shouted. "Captain Sunshine!"

Owen, Kara, and everyone around them looked up into the sky, while some people even started clapping. A man in a yellow superhero suit flew by overhead, waving at the people below. "Keep up the good work, citizens," Captain Sunshine said with a bright smile, and his voice boomed through the streets. People began shouting back compliments and praise.

All in all, this was not *The Dark* comic anymore.

"*That* looked suspiciously like a superhero," Kara said, her eyes on Captain Sunshine as he flew off. "Where exactly are we?"

"I could tell you," Owen told her, "but this is *definitely* some of that nonfictional stuff."

She cringed. "Ugh, fine, I don't want to know."

Now that Captain Sunshine had passed by, the crowds went back to whatever they were doing, though a few children kept laughing and pointing. A strange feeling welled up inside of Owen, and it took him a second to place it. Was this . . . hope? Yes, that was it exactly! *This* was the comic book world Owen had always wanted to visit, not the dark, dystopian nightmare that the Dark had brought about. And just being here seemed to give him a weird feeling of optimism.

Even with Bethany missing, even with the threat of Nobody hanging over him, even with the possibility of the fictional and nonfictional worlds forever separating, Owen couldn't help but smile. And it was all thanks to Jupiter City.

"Okay! We need to find someone named Doc Twilight,"

he told Kara. "Or more specifically, his hideout. Then we can use your time bracelet to go back in time and rescue Bethany from . . ." He paused, realizing he had no idea what *had* happened to her. "Well, we'll see when we get there."

"Sounds easy enough," Kara said. "Any idea where it is?"

"Not even a little bit," Owen said, inwardly wincing. He *would* have, if he'd read forward in the comic page world, instead of investigating Nobody's past.

"What about the guy who just flew off?" Kara asked, nodding into the sky. "He might know this doctor you're looking for. If he doesn't but he really is a superhero, then he probably has vision powers or something and could maybe find the guy for us." She paused. "What's he a doctor of, anyway? Nighttime?"

"Basically," Owen said. "I'd try that, but Captain Sunshine didn't exactly hang around, and I must have left my signal watch at home."

Kara turned him around to point at a sign on a street lamp. "I might know where he's going."

The sign showed Captain Sunshine and other members of the Lawful League standing majestically in front of a domed building.

Come meet the Lawful League

at their headquarters!

Thank them for saving Jupiter City

from the Dark!

Autographs today only from 1–3 p.m.

(No supervillains or evil clones, please.)

"That's so . . . *friendly* of them," Owen said, loving how different this version of Jupiter City was from his last trip. "I guess we need to figure out where the headquarters is?"

"Just a few blocks over, friend!" said a man walking by. He pointed diagonally through a building. "Can't miss it. Just go with the crowds. Everyone's going to be heading over there. They rescued us all from the Dark!"

"Oh, thank you!" Owen said, giving the man a big grin.

"Gotta watch out for each other!" the man said, and tipped a nonexistent hat at Owen before walking off, whistling.

Kara just stared. "Everyone's so weirdly happy and nice," she said, a nervous look on her face. Owen didn't really blame her, honestly. After everything she'd been through, this much light-hearted joy had to seem a bit odd.

The stranger who'd helped them was right: The crowds

14

were mostly heading in the direction of the Lawful Legion event. Following along with Kara, Owen could make out the Apathetic Industries skyscraper that he and Bethany had first appeared in when they'd taken a portal from what turned out to be her sort-of grandfather's house into Jupiter City. Now it was covered in celebratory lighting, cheerfully shining in the midday sun.

As they drew closer, vendors appeared selling balloons covered in superhero symbols, Captain Sunshine ice cream bars, and even some kind of fried fruit pies that promised to stop any hungry supervillain in their tracks. Owen bought one of the pies (while generously tipping the vendor) and bit into it. A rush of goodwill and lawful thoughts filled him, and he loudly *mmm*ed.

Kara giggled at that, then covered her mouth like she was embarrassed. "Whoa, I didn't mean to let that out!" She gave him an apologetic look. "It's hard not to get caught up in the mood here."

"Maybe we can get you superpowers while you're in town?" Owen asked her. "It's not too hard. I got them by accident, and you know how useful they've been."

She laughed again, but this time didn't seem embarrassed by

it. "I'm okay for now, but let me know if you think of some cool ones."

"You could be Time Woman. Or the Clock Queen!"

A cloud passed over her face, and she nodded but turned away. Ugh, why had he reminded her of what she'd left behind? Still, that was the past now. Things here in Jupiter City would be much better for everyone, just as soon as he found Bethany. He weirdly felt so optimistic, what with a fruit pie in his stomach and happy people all around him. What *couldn't* he do right now?

They joined the throngs of people in front of the Lawful Legion's beautiful headquarters. The domed building practically glowed in the sunlight, with white marble rising from a deep green park in front. A pavilion had been set up in the park, but there was only one person onstage.

Owen looked closer, and all of the optimism and joy he felt slowly evaporated. The man onstage was wearing a yellow banana suit.

That was him. The Rotten Banana. The one who'd supposedly been going to take Bethany to the Dark. And apparently had, since the last Owen had seen, the Dark had Bethany in his clutches with the banana nowhere around. Had he turned

Owen's friends over to the Dark, or just abandoned them when things got bad? Neither answer was okay.

"Who wants the Top Banana's autograph?" the banana shouted out into the crowd. "I know, I'm very a-peeling, but there's enough banana in this bunch to go around. Form a line, only twenty bucks a signature!"

Turn to page 335. ◆❯

*P*lease send us home, readers. I don't know if Adelaine really did take your power away, but if not, the Magister is pure evil, and he's probably going to kill us for revenge. Or maybe it's *prevenge*, since he hasn't met me yet. I think?

Readers? Please?

"Come with us, Adelaine," the Magister instructed, then returned to stand before the council. The other members all stood now too and formed a circle with their staffs held high in the air. Adelaine led Owen and Kara off to the side so they wouldn't be in the way, which at least put him farther from the Magister.

The council members began to chant, and their staffs lit up with the same shimmering light as the floor and chairs. From outside, rivers of light began to flow into the center of the room from every conceivable direction, forming a large, swirling ball of energy that hurt Owen's eyes to look at.

More magic-users floated up into the council room from below, while outside the windows, Owen could see another group surrounding the building, all with their staffs raised as well. More explosions filled the air, and the tower shook again, hard enough to almost knock him to his knees.

"YOU HAVE WARPED THE NATURAL LAWS OF OUR WORLD FOR TOO LONG," said a voice over a loudspeaker from outside. "OUR WAR ENDS TODAY. SURRENDER AND FACE YOUR PROPER JUDGMENT."

Adelaine raised her staff, but her glow covered only herself, Owen, and Kara. "I will keep you safe for as long as I am able," she told them. "If I fall, run as far and fast as you can. The Naturalists will know you're not one of them, and will not hesitate to destroy you along with us."

"Who are they?" Kara asked. "And why do they hate you so much?"

"Magic is pure possibility," Adelaine told her, "whereas the Naturalists worship science and control, facts and numbers. As if a human life could ever be encompassed by data. The Naturalists insisted we renounce our 'heathen' spells and use only science. When we refused, they first drove us to the sea, where we formed our own city, Atlantis. But even that wasn't enough for them. Now they insist that we must be wiped from this planet in order to protect themselves." She kneaded her forehead with two fingers. "Fear of the unknown will drive even the bravest to terrible deeds, children."

The building shook again, and the council members began chanting louder. Outside, one of the magic-users screamed, instantly dropping from sight. Owen stepped closer to Kara and grabbed her hand, not even sure why, but somehow feeling better for it.

"It is time!" the Magister shouted. "We need more power, and so turn to those who would be our enemies to provide it. We must take the magic that is their birthright, and use it to build a new reality for all who believe in the infinite!"

One by one, the council members slammed their staffs to the floor, which began to disappear, feeding the ever-growing ball of power in the middle of the room. Owen tapped at Adelaine's bubble frantically. "Um, we're not going to fall when the floor disappears, right? Just want to make sure."

Adelaine shook her head. "I will keep you aloft," she said. "But please, stay quiet. I must lend my power to this endeavor as well."

She tapped her staff on the ground, and now her magic joined the others'.

The conglomerated magic began to fill the room, spreading over and around Owen and Kara, even pushing at the edges of the tower. Another explosion vibrated the walls, which began to crack and crumble.

Then, with one last hit, the tower collapsed around them.

For a moment Owen couldn't see or hear anything beyond the tower's destruction, with rubble tumbling down all around them. But the ball of magic in front of them pushed farther out, sending the remains of the tower flying off in all directions and leaving them all floating in midair.

Strangely, many of those pieces of the former tower changed course as they flew and crashed into large metal tanks that now filled the city streets. Apparently someone guided them as a last-ditch attack. Owen looked closer at the tanks and realized they were the boats he'd seen before, but transformed somehow. Technology here was so much more advanced than in his world! Maybe the TSA's time bracelets had it beat, but he'd never seen anything like these war machines. Each one had a variety of different weapons and seemed to be using them all at once. The magic-users still defending the city were hopelessly overmatched, and now the tanks were releasing soldiers encased in some kind of metal suits into the fray.

"Take their magic!" the Magister shouted, and a powerful wave of force swept out of the council members in every direction. At first nothing happened, but then a few stray trickles of light began to feed into the magic filling the air, coming from the soldiers in the metal suits. More and more streams joined together, forming large rivers of magic that flowed into the room from all directions. Larger rivers began to flow out of the war machines, and great floods came crashing in from the horizon in all directions.

The magic surrounding them now grew even bigger, and it wasn't just shimmering light anymore. Inside the magical sphere Owen could see what looked like stars, galaxies, nebulas—all the things he'd seen in pictures of space but had never really understood.

The magicians really were creating a new universe, a reality built from pure possibility. It was truly awesome to stand in the middle of it all, and for a moment all of Owen's worries fell away, and he just marveled at the sight.

A strike from a war machine yanked his attention back to reality as a blast exploded into the side of the magic, sending sizzles throughout the entire newly forming universe. A few sparks of magic burst out, and one passed through Owen, making his hair rise on end and filling his head with strange thoughts about flying elephant donkeys making popcorn.

Apparently pure possibility led to some *odd* ideas.

"We will build a new world, just like our home," the Magister said, and a new planet began to form in the vastness of space in the middle of the magic. "But we will not stop there. Every possibility will exist in this universe, an infinite reality unlike anything that has ever existed. We twelve will build thousands upon thousands of new worlds, and our descendants will do the same, adding to our universe until it becomes truly never-ending."

The planet that the council had just built began to shimmer, and in its place there were now two, then four, then sixteen planets, some exactly alike, others vastly different. Soon there were more planets than Owen could count, with more shimmering into view with every passing second.

"The time has come!" the Magister shouted as magic-users defending them began to fall left and right, and the war machines started rising in the air like hovercrafts, floating up to their height. "Choose your new existence, and leave this one behind!"

Each of the council members raised their staffs and floated up into one of the new worlds, leaving many, many more empty. Adelaine nodded down at Kara and Owen, her face looking much more haggard than it had before. She floated their bubble into one of the original four planets, the same one the Magister was approaching. "Don't worry if this isn't the reality you know," she said, sounding exhausted. "We have planned for this. There will be methods to travel between each one, and we will find your home reality for you."

"The boy's home reality?" the Magister said, glancing at Owen as they flew toward a new planet. "But that would be the world we just left."

Owen's eyebrows shot up. He must have misheard that. He *had* to have misheard that. The planet with the Naturalists and Atlantis and magic and technology beyond anything he'd ever seen . . . that was his world? His Earth? His reality?

Turn to page 286. ⬍⟩

Owen took a step back in shock, but Kara rushed forward and grabbed his older self by the shirt. "How old are you now?" she demanded, her face a mix of panic and terror. "*Owen*, tell me! What year is this? *How old are you?*"

Owen's future self put his hands on her shoulders and gave her a sad smile. "Hi, Kara. It's going to be okay. Just breathe."

Kara shook her head over and over. "When is this? I need to know! It might not be too late—"

"We can't do this here," older Owen said, gesturing for Owen to come. He pulled Kara with him, and Owen followed himself past the statue of the Countess and into a nearby alley. His future self opened an unmarked door, then walked them through a kitchen filled with people cooking, washing dishes, and plating orders. No one even looked at them.

Instead of going out into the restaurant, older Owen led

them down some stairs and into a storeroom. There he flipped a light switch off and on three times. After the third time, a pile of boxes silently glided aside, revealing a lit hallway behind it.

"When the Countess took over, we had to find a way to stay out of sight," older Owen said, leading Owen and Kara down the hallway. They passed by several doors, behind a few of which Owen could hear people talking. "We rescued who we could, but the Countess was very thorough." He pointed at a partway open door, through which they could see rows of desks about half-filled with people poring over books. "We've got agents documenting every appearance of the Countess throughout history. When we're ready, we plan on striking each point simultaneously, and—"

Kara shoved him against the hallway wall. "Tell me *when I am*, Owen!"

Owen tried to pull her off of his older self, but future Owen just put a hand up, stopping him. "It's okay," he said to Owen. "You . . . you don't know what's happening here yet, and if I can help it, you never will. But Kara has questions, and she deserves some answers. Owen, would you mind waiting for a few minutes?" He opened a nearby door and gestured for Owen to go in.

"What? No way!" Owen shouted. "I've got questions too! First of all, why are you here? Did we never get back to Bethany? Did Nobody separate the worlds? And how does Kara know me when I've never met her?"

Older Owen waited for him to finish. "Is that all?"

"Not even close," Owen shouted again, then took a deep breath to calm down. "How did the Countess change the entire world? Where did the time prison go? And why are you still here?!"

"You asked that already," Kara told him, absently staring at his older self.

"It's a really important question," Owen told her.

"Fine, Owen first," future Owen said. Kara started to object, but he shook his head. "*Then* I tell you everything I can, okay? He's not going to give us time until he gets some information too." He gave Owen an intent look. "But before we start, I need to keep *you* in control here. So we're going to fix a little, um, let's call it a problem you've been having since you woke up in the prison, okay?"

"A problem?" Owen asked, but his older self just winked. Oh, great. Apparently he was going to start thinking he was Kiel in the future. Ugh.

"In here," older Owen said, and led them into the same room he'd tried to push Owen into earlier. He closed the door behind them, then waved at a cot for Owen and Kara to sit down. Future Owen, meanwhile, grabbed a chair from a small desk and flipped it around before sitting down.

Wow. Did he think that was cool or something?

"First of all, this *is* cool," Owen's older self told him. Owen's eyes widened, and the future version laughed. "Don't worry, I can't read your mind. I just know how you think. For example, right now you're thinking that it's annoying that I called you on it."

Owen glared at his older self, not willing to admit he was right. "So? What's this problem you're going to fix?"

Older Owen glanced at Kara, then turned back to Owen. "Remember how you got the exit code in spite of not being able to remember it?" He raised an eyebrow. "And how sometimes things happen that you don't choose yourself? Well, I'm going to fix that for you."

Huh? Was he talking about the readers? He could *fix* that? But how?

"I knew you'd end up here," older Owen said while he fished around in his pocket, looking for something. "You know, since

I did too, so many years ago. But when I got here, and the older me tried to teach me something, Kara and I immediately, um, got pulled away." He winked again at Owen, trying much too hard to make his point without saying it out loud. Owen rolled his eyes. "So I had over a decade to figure out how to fix that. Not to mention a few other things. But first, let's make sure you don't disappear suddenly." His future self took something from his pocket, then rose from his chair and came over to Owen. "Close your eyes. It's probably better that you don't see this. You too, Kara."

Owen gave himself a suspicious look, but closed his eyes as requested . . . then opened them just a bit. He couldn't make out much, but from what he could tell, it almost looked like his older self held a piece of paper in his hand.

"I said *close* them," his older self said, and smacked Owen's head. Owen mumbled some choice words but scrunched his eyes shut. He felt his older self touch his forehead, then heard him mumble something in a different language. "Okay, done."

Owen's eyes flew open. He didn't *feel* any different necessarily, but still, somehow he knew things had changed. "What did you *do* to me?" he demanded.

"Oh, calm down, it was just a quick magic spell."

"A *what*, now?"

"It won't hurt you."

"How do I know that?"

"Because I'm *you*. If I did it to you, I'd have hurt me too!"

"Boys, can we get past this?" Kara asked, shaking her head. "I have important things *I* need to know."

Owen's older self leaned down so his mouth was near Owen's ear. "A few years ago I went back to the beginning of the fictional universe and saw how it was created. Basically, magic used to exist on our world, but a bunch of people feared it, so the magicians built a new reality to escape to. I know, it's basically the Kiel Gnomenfoot books. There's a reason for that. But you'll see when you go back in time yourself." He seemed to realize he was going on for too long, because he shook his head. "Anyway, one of the magicians used that spell on me, and I made sure to make a copy so I could use it on you when the time came."

"And the spell did what?"

"It'll keep any outside forces from influencing your decisions," his older self said carefully, glancing quickly at Kara. "At least until you decide you want them back."

~~WHAT? IS HE SAYING HE TOOK AWAY OUR~~
~~CHOICE HERE? FORGET THAT! OWEN~~
~~PUNCHES HIS OLDER SELF IN THE FACE.~~
~~Turn to page~~ ███ . ⬍⟩

Like any magic spell could keep the readers from deciding what happened, but whatever. "We'll see if it works," Owen said, needing more answers. "So back to my questions. Are you stuck here? Does that mean I never get back to Bethany either? Does Nobody separate the worlds?"

Older Owen sighed. "Yes. I could never get back to Jupiter City, and it does appear as if Nobody removed all of the portals." He paused, then leaned in so Kara couldn't hear. "Even worse, once he separates the worlds, things here become . . . less anchored. The fictional world falls apart. I've seen it in the future . . . it's just like the space outside of stories, only that's all that exists anymore." He stood. "But it's not too late to fix this."

"How?" Owen asked quietly, not looking at his older self. Nobody had found Bethany, all because Owen had never escaped from Kara's book. He failed Bethany, he failed all of their friends, and he failed two entire worlds.

Future Owen moved closer. "Because I've spent the last

31

decade working on a way for *you* to fix it for both of us. Something that my older self tried to teach me, but like I said, we left too soon. I can't fix things, because if I did, that'd cause a paradox, and my Kara's not here to protect us from it. But *you* can! You can change everything now, because look what I finally figured out how to do!"

And with that, Owen's older self reached into thin air, grabbed nothing, then yanked down, tearing a page in the middle of the room. On the other side of the torn page an enormous dragon frowned at them, then licked its lips.

"I know how to travel between stories now, Owen," future Owen said, quickly shutting the page before the dragon could eat them. "And I can teach you to do it too!"

~~THIS CAN'T BE REAL. OWEN CHOOSES TO DANCE AROUND RIDICULOUSLY, JUST TO PROVE WE CAN STILL DECIDE THINGS.~~

~~Turn to page~~ ████. ⬍❯

WOW, THE SPELL REALLY DID WORK, DIDN'T IT? WE DON'T REALLY HAVE A CHOICE.

Turn to page 143. ⬍❯

unich in the year 4120," Kara said, grabbing Owen's hand and hitting the bracelet.

They jumped forward in time, only to appear in the middle of nothing. Everything was just blank, a white world absent of anything, just like the space between stories.

"Wait, what happened?" Kara said. "The time bracelet says we're in the correct year, but this can't be the same place."

What did this mean? The world was just . . . gone. Had Nobody split the fictional and nonfictional worlds, and this was the result?

"Something's *very* wrong," Kara said.

"It sure is," said a voice, and they whirled around to find Dolores with several robed guards. She immediately touched Owen and Kara on the neck, and they both collapsed to the ground.

The last thing Owen heard was Dolores's voice getting farther and farther away. "Bring them, but keep them asleep. The Countess doesn't want them to wake up before she disposes of them."

Readers, turn back now! This is the . . . the wrong . . .

And then everything went dark.

So time is moving backward," Kara said, pointing at the lava flowing upward. "But how did we get here? And where *is* here exactly?"

From the top of the mountain Owen could see a vast jungle laid out before them. As the lava retreated back up toward a large fissure near where they were standing, it revealed what looked like a path leading . . . somewhere. A few pterodactyls flew lazily through the air in reverse, their tails leading the way as they reverse hunted. He watched as one vomited up a small lizard of some kind, held it in its mouth for a moment, then dove with it backward to the ground, and deposited it there safely before reversing its dive back into the air.

"This is going to be odd, isn't it," he whispered to himself.

"Which is pretty much our normal, huh?" Kara said, bumping him with her shoulder. "After the lava all goes back into the volcano, let's go check out that path. Maybe it leads back to the air lock?"

Owen nodded, having no idea what was going on. How could time be moving backward all around them, but they were still living forward? Was this really the outside, or was it just made up to look that way? Charm would have been able to figure this out in a matter of seconds. Why couldn't Nobody have thrown the half-robotic girl in here with him?

As the last of the lava climbed up the mountain, leaving uneven rocks in its wake, something began to sizzle next to them, right in the lava's path. As they watched, a metal sign-post unmelted out of the lava, and slowly rose into the air. Scorch marks gradually disappeared, leaving behind the words TAKE ME in large letters.

Great. Like that kind of thing never got Alice in trouble in Wonderland.

"I guess we take it?" Kara asked, waiting until the lava had cleared the sign before yanking it out of the rock. The fully restored sign still didn't look very new, and the words were faded into the metal as if from weather. Owen sighed. Maybe it'd become less weathered as they continued on, if time kept being all ridiculous.

"So what, now we just try out the path?" he asked, not liking their options.

"Yes, and fast," Kara told him, pointing at the pterodactyls. "I think we've been spotted. Though it's a bit hard to tell, since that one's flying toward us backward."

She was right, one of the largest dinosaurs was soaring right at them tail-first. "Run!" Owen shouted, and followed Kara down the rocky mountainside.

Keeping their footing turned out to be a lot harder than it looked. The entire volcano was now covered in loose gravel and rocks, and half the time it felt more like they were sliding or surfing down than running. Even worse, as they got farther down the mountain, the pterodactyl began to dive, looking to land right in the same spot they were heading for.

"Hold up!" Kara shouted, and braced herself against the rocks, trying to slow her progress. Owen grabbed her arm, and together they slid to a stop just as the creature's tail came flying right for them. The dinosaur snapped its jaws just in front of Kara's lead foot, then abruptly changed direction and took off into the air backward, shrieking loud enough to send a chill through Owen.

"It's hunting us backward," Kara said. "Somehow its time line is still connected to ours. We're going to have to be really careful."

Owen watched as the pterodactyl flew away, apparently not interested in taking another shot. Or wait, it wouldn't be another shot, it'd have been a first shot? Maybe? His brain began to pound just trying to wrap his head around it.

They reached the bottom of the mountain without any further incidents and slowly approached the path. The jungle covered so much of the land that it was impossible to see more than ten or so feet down the pathway, so anything could be out there.

"Do you hear that?" Kara asked, holding up a hand to stop him.

He paused, and could just make out some kind of metal crunching noise. Whatever it was, it didn't sound particularly friendly. But the jungle surrounding the volcano was far too thick to make their way through, so the path seemed like the only option. "Sounds like we're going to regret this challenge," he said to Kara. "Ready?"

She forced a smile and led the way along the path. Just a few feet after the volcano disappeared behind them, they saw the source of the metallic noises: a Tyrannosaurus rex was slowly uneating TIME-R.

Kara pushed Owen out of the way behind a tree, then

looked back around the bend. "That's so *disgusting*," she whispered. "I hope this didn't happen because I said it should!"

Something began to beep, and Owen pushed up next to her to see. The T. rex had just put back into place a piece of TIME-R's head, and the robot's eyes had lit up. It seemed dazed still and was repeating a phrase over and over. "SOMERSVILLE. HOUGH STREET. JUNE FIRST, 2054. ONE THIRTY-FIVE P.M. SOMERSVILLE. HOUGH STREET. JUNE FIRST, 2054. ONE THIRTY-FIVE P.M."

"What's it saying?" Owen whispered to Kara.

She shrugged. "A date and location important to it, maybe? Could be when it was first built?"

Owen went cold. "Or maybe when it founded the TSA."

Another backward bite, and the robot's head was now completely restored. It stopped repeating the phrase, then seemed to see the dinosaur slowly uneating it for the first time. "THIS IS UNEXPECTED," it said.

"I think the T. rex is almost done eating him," Kara said. "Or almost to the point where it started. There's just a leg missing now."

And as she said it, the dinosaur regurgitated up a robot leg, attaching it back into place.

"HUMANS," TIME-R shouted at them. "IF I UNDER-STAND WHAT IS HAPPENING HERE, I SUGGEST YOU NOW COME OVER HERE. HURRY!"

Uh, what now? Join him in getting eaten? There was no way that was going to happen!

DO WHAT THE ROBOT SAYS!

Turn to page 358. ⬦❯

UM, GO TOWARD THE DINOSAUR?
THAT'LL GET OWEN KILLED. JUST
STAY THERE AND WAIT!

Turn to page 186. ⬦❯

x

I'm going to distract that thing," Kara said, readying herself to run back the way they'd come. "You find the exit code, okay?"

"What?" Owen said. "There's no way—"

"I'll be fine!" she said. "Whatever happens here will be reset at midnight. Now just go, okay? I'm not letting you get hurt if I have any say in the matter!"

With one last look, she turned to run back toward the T. rex.

Then she froze as soon as her hand left Owen's.

In spite of everything, he had to smile at that.

He grabbed her hand again, speeding her time back up. "I'm pretty sure that's not going to work."

"Oh!" she said, staring at his hand and turning bright red. "Um. Right."

"Any other ideas?" Owen asked.

**HAVE KARA SUGGEST THAT THEY
CROSS THE RAVINE JUST AHEAD.**

Turn to page 214. ⬍❯

There was no loud, pounding thought that answered his request, so Owen had no idea if the readers had even heard him. Unfortunately, Kara didn't seem to be having much luck as she kept pushing symbol after symbol on the time bracelet.

He gritted his teeth and turned away so she couldn't see him, then stared out at the nothingness, hoping he was looking readers directly in the eye.

Hey, everyone out there. I know we didn't get off on the right foot. You tried to control me and make me do things that I didn't want to do, and I . . . well, I never did anything to you. I get that if you believe what Nobody says, that nonfictional people control you somehow . . . well then, you probably don't like me much. But please, don't take that out on Kara. And doubly don't take that out on Bethany. She's half-fictional herself, and she's done nothing but try to find her father. And look what happened when she did. Please. Help us here, and send me back to Bethany, and I'll promise to tell every single nonfictional writer exactly what they're doing. I'll start petitions, I'll e-mail the president, whatever it takes! Just please . . . help us?

He squeezed his eyes closed, hoping that when he opened them, the bracelet would be fixed, and they'd be on their way to the present, at which point the readers would rip a page in space in front of him between stories, and he could step back into the world of Jupiter City to find Bethany. *Please?* Owen thought one last time. Then he took a deep breath and opened his eyes.

"Wow, I think I made it worse," Kara said. "*That's* unfortu-nate."

Oh, GREAT. Thanks a lot, readers! You're a huge help all around. So now you're trying to kill me and *one of your own fictional people? Perfect. Hope you're enjoying this, Nobody. Because these readers are being worse than authors ever would be. At least authors give their characters a way out of hopeless situations!*

"There might be a way out, though," Kara said, looking off in the direction of the big bang. "It could kill us even faster if it doesn't work, but what's a few extra minutes of life worth, anyway?"

"Um, a lot?" Owen said, wondering how long he could survive in the vacuum of space if he just let go of her hand right now and took his chances. "What's the idea?"

"I can't get us moving forward in time again, not without stopping the bracelet for a few minutes to reset it," she said. "And we wouldn't last ten seconds out here, let alone long enough for it to reboot."

Okay, *yikes*. Ten seconds was definitely worse than a few minutes. Owen tightened his grip. "So what's the idea, then?"

"What if I make us go backward even faster?"

". . . Faster."

"Yeah!" She actually seemed excited by this. "As fast as we can."

"You want to send us hurtling toward the big bang, where we'll get crunched into nothingness, dying instantly . . . *quicker*."

She shoved her shoulder against his. "You must not see the benefits of the plan."

"Not really, no."

"Well, to be fair, I'm not entirely sure there are any," she said, which didn't really help Owen's growing feeling of dread. "But here's the thing. If we can get going fast enough, I think we can

45

use our momentum to catch the big bang's event horizon like a whirlpool, and have it shoot us out the other direction. Which in this case might be nothingness."

"Nothingness?!"

"But," Kara continued quickly, "there are theories that other realities existed *before* the big bang. Some people even think that a previous version of humanity eventually became evolved enough to create a universe itself, and that's what the big bang was. So if we can just pass through into that universe, we could be okay!"

"I heard a lot of 'theories' in there," Owen said, his knees starting to shake from terror. "Why did the time bracelet have to break, huh?" He turned his head out to space. "Seriously! Why couldn't *whoever's in charge here* just let you fix the bracelet? Or even just have a spaceship come along and save us? There are literally an infinite number of possible ways we could have been saved, and yet, somehow we're still going to die. Does that seem fair to you people?!"

"I can see you're busy ranting, so I'm just going to try it," Kara said, and hit a symbol. Instantly, the stars began flowing toward the big bang even faster, and the universe started to darken.

"What? No!" Owen shouted.

"This is our only chance, Owen," Kara said, quickly tapping a symbol a few more times. Time sped backward now too fast for Owen to even see individual stars. It was like hitting warp drive in every movie or TV show ever, just lines of light all heading in one direction . . . toward the big bang.

"We're heading into *nothing*," he yelled at her. "Nothing means that there's nothing there. There's nothing in nothing! And once we're in nothing, *we'll* be nothing!"

She gave him a sad look. "At least this way there's a chance. And if it doesn't work . . . then I guess destiny isn't as all-powerful as it seems."

What? *Wait a second.* "*That's* what this is about?" Owen said.

"That's what it's always about," Kara whispered, and grabbed his arm with hers, holding it tightly.

Owen growled in frustration. "*Fine.* I hope that anyone out there who can see us right now feels *very guilty* about all of this!"

"You and your nonfictional stuff," she said, giving him a smile as the lines of light outside began to wink out, with fewer remaining each second. From thousands to hundreds, to just dozens. Then five. Four. Three. Two. One.

Finally, the last line of light sped past, and that was it. There was only blackness.

And then a wall of pure nothing came rushing toward them, encompassing all of existence. A wall that didn't even look like the blackness of space, it was just . . . the end of everything. Just like in that Kiel Gnomenfoot book. "If Kiel survived it, maybe we can too," Owen whispered.

"Who's Kiel?" Kara asked, and Owen felt her hand tremble.

"Someone I wish were here right now," Owen told her. "You know, for what it's worth, I *really* don't want to die."

Kara nodded, not looking at him. "You have no idea how much I agree with that. It's my fault, Owen, I know. It's *always* my fault. I can't escape it."

The wall of nothing drew closer, and Owen closed his eyes, taking a deep breath. *I'm so sorry, Bethany. I did my best to get back to you, but time travel is just the* worst. *I hope someday you get to read this, and maybe you can track down all the readers who sent us in this direction and throw* them *into a Pick the Plot book. Would serve them right.*

"Here it comes!" Kara shouted, and Owen began to scream. Kara joined in, then reached out and hugged him close as the wall of nothingness slammed into them with the force of all reality.

And after that, there was only nothing.

UH-OH. LET'S MAYBE GO BACK AND TRY THE FUTURE ROUTE INSTEAD.

Turn to page 206. ⬍❯

WAIT. IS THERE ANYTHING *IN* THE NOTHINGNESS? LET'S JUST TAKE A LOOK.

Turn to page 230. ⬍❯

The Jupiter Hill Observatory topped what Owen assumed was Jupiter Hill, where it looked like a war had occurred. The ground was ripped up all over the place, and a large broken crystal shield seemed to be embedded in the dirt so deeply that the construction crews fixing things were removing it with a crane.

"Sorry, kids, this is a hard hat area only," said one of the construction workers as they approached. "Observatory is closed until we get things cleaned up here. Shouldn't be more than a day or so." He grinned. "This actually isn't even that bad. Did you see the invasion of the atomic universe two years ago? Tiny people, but wow did they pack a punch. Only took us a week to rebuild the entire city, but those were some long nights!"

"We really need to get in there," Owen said, looking

around for another entrance. "Isn't there some way we can sneak by?"

The man laughed and ruffled Owen's hair in a way that did not help his mood at all. "Nice try. I like your gumption, especially in front of the young lady here." Kara blushed, and Owen raised his hands to object, but the man continued, "Like I said, it's a hard hat area only. And safety is our number one concern."

"So . . . can we just put on hard hats, then?" Kara asked.

He stared at her for a moment, then shrugged. "Looks like you found a loophole, miss!" He grabbed two hard hats from a box next to the entrance and handed them over. "Now, be sure to keep those on while you're in there, or I'll have to escort you out. And keep an eye out for that crane, will you? We've dropped Rock 'n' Roll's crystal shield a few times now. A lot heavier than it looks, and it looks plenty heavy!"

Owen sighed as he put on the hard hat, then led the way up the battlefield toward the observatory door. The climb up the hill actually was more treacherous than it looked from below, given all the craters in the dirt and various leftovers from superpowers. But the construction workers seemed to know what they were doing, flattening the land back down and laying sod over it. Comic book cities got destroyed all the time, so it made sense that someone would have to rebuild them. Probably good work for a construction company.

They kept moving and were approaching the entrance to the observatory when Owen stepped on something squishy. He lost his balance and tumbled to the ground as the squishy thing spoke up. "Hey! Watch where you're stepping!" said . . . whatever it was.

Kara reached down and helped what looked exactly like a person made of dirt stand up. The dirt faded away, leaving an annoyed-looking man in some sort of military camouflage.

"Are you okay?" Kara asked, and the man yanked his arm away from her.

"No, I'm *not* okay!" he shouted, glaring at Owen. "He stepped right on me!"

"I'm so sorry," Owen said, pushing to his feet. "Why were you lying there?"

"Mr. Sleep hit me with his magic sand after he got turned evil by the Dark," the man said, brushing actual dirt off himself while looking around. "How long have I been here? And why didn't anyone wake me up before now?!"

"I'm not sure they could see you," Kara pointed out.

The man groaned. "I tell you, this camouflage has done me more harm than good. It might be time to give up my mastery of the world's greatest stealth system secrets and just go back to being a dentist. My dad used to tell me that was good work, you know?"

"Look, it's Smokescreen!" one of the construction workers said. "Someone call for a doctor!"

"I'm fine, no thanks to you guys," the man shouted back.

"Smokescreen?" Kara asked. "Why not something like the Chameleon?"

"Because this suit has the power, and it looks like camouflage, so I had to go with something military-sounding, okay?" Smokescreen told her. "No one's around when you try to brainstorm names, but once you pick one, everyone's got an opinion."

Owen pulled Kara away from the man, who moved his complaining to the construction workers. "We should just let him be, I think," he whispered to Kara, who nodded.

The observatory entrance wasn't far, fortunately, because Smokescreen's voice definitely traveled. It looked like the doors had been blown off the building, though one had already been replaced. They slipped in through the empty spot where the second door had been and found themselves in a dark, round room lit only by computers.

"This looks a lot more like an actual observatory than a hideout," Kara said. "You think this is the right place?"

"I hope so," Owen told her. "It's not like I trust the banana man. But who knows when the Lawful Legion will be done with the giant toad monster, so we should at least check this out in the meantime. Maybe there's a secret way in to Doc Twilight's headquarters?"

Kara clicked on the light switch, and they both searched the room. Somehow it had avoided a lot of the damage of the battle, though here and there some of the computer monitors were broken, and a few of the walls had burn marks. A giant telescope filled most of the room, and a computer screen below it showed a map of the night sky.

Hmm. Doc Twilight had a moon and stars on his costume. He wouldn't have made the secret entrance to his headquarters open by using the telescope, would he? Was that too obvious?

Owen moved over to the computer and typed in a location, then watched as the giant telescope rotated around.

54

"Where'd you aim it?" Kara asked, coming over to him.

"Jupiter," Owen said. "Since this place is named Jupiter City, I figured it was worth a shot." He folded his arms, inwardly smiling. If this worked, he was about to look *awesome*.

The telescope stopped at Jupiter, but nothing happened. Owen frowned, then tapped the map on the computer screen again. "Maybe it's broken or something."

"What did you say his name was again?" Kara asked, staring at the night sky map.

"Doc Twilight."

She nodded, then tapped in different coordinates. The telescope moved again, and this time when it stopped, the wall behind it disappeared, revealing stairs leading down into darkness.

Owen looked at Kara in shock, and she just smiled back. "Where did *you* point it?"

"The moon," she said. "That's the only thing you see at twilight. The stars haven't really come out yet, but the moon is visible."

"That's . . . genius."

She blushed. "Jupiter made sense too. Come on. Let's go

downstairs before I say something to ruin things."

Owen smiled, then walked after her toward the staircase. There didn't seem to be a light, so they began climbing down slowly, hoping their eyes would adjust.

Unfortunately, they didn't. Not before the attack came.

Turn to page 150. ⬦❯

ut how are you doing this?" Owen asked. The bald woman covered his mouth with her hand, glaring at him to keep silent. She and the Countess started dragging them toward the exit door, holding each other's free hand at the same time.

"One scream, even one word from either of you, and the other one dies," the Countess whispered to them, and Kara gave her a look that would have knocked over an ordinary person. The Countess just smiled in response, and they made it through the open exit door without being detected.

On the other side was a room about the size of a large closet. Two chairs sat next to a small circular table, and a number of bracelets were plugged into some kind of electronic device on the wall. Unfortunately, that was it. There was nothing that could be used as a weapon, or even a distraction, to get away from the Countess. This was *not* good.

The bald woman slowly closed the door, then clicked a button on an electronic pad to the side. The exit door loudly locked, which made Owen jump, figuring they were caught for sure. But neither the time agents nor anyone else came barging in.

The agents had to know the exit code, right? Otherwise they were in for a *long* day at the prison.

"You asked how we did that?" the bald woman said to Owen, standing over him with her arms crossed. "You think I don't know about *you*, Owen Conners? I've studied your whole life, you and Kara both. You're my mother's greatest enemies, after all. And because of you two, I almost didn't exist."

"What are you talking about?" Owen said. "There's no way you could have studied me, my life." How could she, from inside a book?

The bald woman stepped closer, then held up her hand to Owen's face as it began to vibrate faster and faster.

"Recognize your power, kid?" she asked. "Took me decades of research, but I've re-created it, even made it better. I can slow time down in other objects . . . or speed it up until they explode." She held her hand closer to Owen's face, and he flinched away.

The Countess rolled her eyes. "*Enough*, Dolores. You never know when to end your ramblings."

The bald woman looked like she'd been struck. "Yes, Mother," she said. "I apologize."

"As you should," the Countess said, and turned back to Kara. "Now I believe we have a matter to discuss, Kara Dox. After all, you reneged on our deal." She held up her glowing glove and brought it close to Kara's face, just as Dolores had done to Owen. "Not to mention you said some very *nasty* things to me a few minutes ago. Maybe I'll give you a taste of your older years, shall I?"

"Turn her to dust, Mother!" the bald woman shouted.

"Silence, Dolores!" the Countess said, turning away from Kara. "Children should speak only when spoken to!"

Again, the bald woman looked hurt, but this time, she didn't apologize.

While the Countess was distracted, Kara leaped for the door back into the prison, but Dolores grabbed her, locking her arms through Kara's armpits and threading her fingers around the back of her neck.

"Let me *go!*" Kara shouted, her face pointed at the floor. "I have to get back in the prison. If I never leave, I won't be able to stop you. You'll be free, don't you get it?"

"Stop talking, you little monster," Dolores said, pushing Kara's neck forward until she yelped in pain. "You're going to wish you'd never been born by the time we're—"

"Dolores!" the Countess roared. "Must you ruin every victory with your incessant prattle? I am trying to keep a dignified air here, but you can't help yourself, can you?"

"Mother, I just hate them *so much*—"

"Speak again, and you'll feel the glove as well," the Countess hissed.

Yikes. Owen took a step away from the two women. This was going badly in *so* many ways (not the least of which was this incredibly awkward mother-daughter relationship). With the Countess's glove and Dolores's powers, fighting back was far too dangerous. But if the Countess meant to kill them anyway, it was better than nothing.

Owen glanced over at Kara as Dolores released her hold a bit, turning to apologize again to her mother. Kara caught his eye, turned her gaze on the bracelets, then back to Owen. Were those important in some way? Something they could use for protection?

"This is why your father hated you!" the Countess told her daughter, her gloved hand clenched in a fist. "I'm locked away in time prison, and what's your brilliant plan to rescue me? You get locked away too! Never in time was a child more useless to her mother!"

"I thought I could be helpful!" Dolores said as Owen inched toward the bracelets on the wall.

"*Helpful?* You've been disappointing me since the day you were born. Why change the habit of a lifetime?"

Owen leaned back against the charging device, then slowly lifted an arm behind his back, trying to reach for a bracelet. He snagged one in his fingers, but it slipped and dropped to the cement floor with a loud, rubbery smack.

The Countess and Dolores both turned at the noise. "And what exactly do *you* think you're doing?" the Countess asked him.

"He was going for a time bracelet!" Dolores said, pointing at the charging device.

"You *filth*," the Countess said, practically spitting it out. "I grant you several minutes of extra life before I turn you to dust, and this is how you repay me?" She stepped toward him, her glowing glove outstretched.

"Bill me?" Owen whispered to himself, then stood still, hoping this was going to work.

The Countess snarled, then lunged out at him with her hand. Owen dropped to the ground, letting her hand hit the wall, which began immediately to decay. He grabbed the bracelet from the floor, pushed whatever buttons on it he could, then slipped it around the Countess's ankle, locking it in place.

"Bill me!" he shouted, loud enough for everyone to hear this time. And then he waited.

Just like with the exit door, nothing happened. "You didn't turn it *on*," the woman said, starting to smile.

"That's okay," Kara said, kicking the bracelet hard at the Countess's side. "That's what he's got me for."

The Countess opened her mouth to scream, but instead disappeared into thin air.

"Mother!" Dolores shouted, grabbing a bracelet from the wall and pushing its buttons. "Where did you send her, you horrible creature? *Tell me!*"

"I honestly have no idea," Owen said, spreading his hands.

"I'll find you," Dolores said, baring her teeth at him. "No

matter where you run, no matter where you hide, and—"

"Don't you want to go find your mother?" Kara asked.

Dolores jumped as if slapped, then hit her own bracelet and disappeared.

Kara jumped toward Owen, hugging him tightly. "You did it!" she shouted. "I meant for you to put one on yourself and get out of here, but that worked too!" She pulled away, then grabbed another bracelet and pushed a few buttons. "There's no time to waste, though. The time prison's protective fields make exact time jumps in here impossible, but they'll find a way back at least within the next ten minutes or so. You need to go get help, to protect you from the Countess and her daughter." She grinned shyly. "Maybe try me last year? That's when I first met *you*, after all."

Owen put the bracelet on his wrist, then held out his hand to her. "Come with me. You can't stay here. I don't care what you did or are going to do; this is no way to deal with it."

She looked away for a moment, then shook her head. "The entire timestream will suffer if I'm free. I can't. I just *can't*."

Kara took a step toward the door back into the prison, then turned and looked back. "Push that red button and you'll be taken right where you need to go. Say hi to me a year ago, okay? And have fun, you two. *We* definitely did."

And with that, she put her hand up to the code box to unlock the door. Only, before she could touch it, the code box disappeared. As did the door, the closet-sized room, and the entire prison.

Instead, Owen and Kara found themselves standing in the middle of a very loud, very prehistoric jungle, with no signs that the time prison had ever even existed.

HUH? WHERE'D THE PRISON GO?

Turn to page 196. ⬍❯

*I*T'S A TRICK. JUMP INTO THE LAVA, IT'S THE ONLY WAY TO PROVE THIS ISN'T REAL!

The thought smacked Owen hard enough in the face that he moved before realizing what he was doing. He crouched, ready to leap . . . and then knocked himself to the ground.

Are you trying to kill me?! he shouted at the readers. *I'm not jumping into lava. I don't care if it's a trick or not!*

"Are you okay?" Kara said, running to his side. "What happened?"

Owen just shook his head. "You really don't want to know."

Look, he thought. *If it's not real, there's a less lethal way to find that out. Can we just look around for now? Is that too much to ask, for a few extra minutes of life?*

He carefully pushed to his feet, bracing against any further thoughts about jumping into the lava, but none seemed to come. Okay, this was good. Time to find out what was actually happening.

FINE. FIND OUT WHAT HAPPENED, IF IT'S SO IMPORTANT TO YOU.

Turn to page 35.

Sitting with their backs up against the cottage, Kara turned to Owen. "You're going to find this all out when *I* first meet *you*," she said, "but I got a time bracelet from my twenty-five-year-old self. She showed up in the middle of my bedroom and, like, collapsed on the spot. She barely made it back to me alive." She took a deep breath. "She gave me the bracelet and told me what was going to happen, Owen. She said that only I could fix it. But she was wrong."

"What did she tell you?"

"Four things would happen," Kara said, counting them off on her fingers. "First, I would cause the entire Time Security Agency to not exist. Check. Second, I'd unleash the greatest evil the world has ever known into the timestream. Also check. Third, my best friend would . . . sacrifice himself to save me." She paused, not looking at him. "And last, all of reality would cease to exist."

Owen's mouth dropped open. "That's . . . a lot to take in."

"Especially since I'd never heard of time travel before that point," Kara told him, picking some grass and tossing it into the breeze. "At first I thought it was so cool, and that I could easily keep all of those things from happening. But the more I saw of the future, the more I realized none of it was changing. We couldn't even . . . my future selves always failed to save . . ."

Owen started to blush. "You're talking about—"

She nodded, not looking at him. "I figured that if this was all my fault, that maybe locking myself away in time prison would keep it from happening. But look what that got me!" She banged her fist on the cottage wall hard enough to shake it. "Instead of avoiding my destiny, I caused it myself! Not in the same way as my future selves did either. I made sure *not* to make their mistakes, but it doesn't matter . . . the same things keep happening no matter what I do. And now look! The Countess kept the TSA from being created, and I unleashed her on the timestream again." She turned to look at him, rubbing her forearm over her wet eyes. "And we know what comes next."

Owen felt a chill go through his body, and he shivered in the warm sunlight. "Well, um, we'll just make sure that doesn't happen, then."

"It *always* happens!" she shouted, leaping to her feet. "Everyone else in the world gets to have a future that's completely open, a future that hasn't happened yet. But not me. I have to be the one person immune to paradox, which means I *can't* change my future. While the entire world changes around me, my time line is set in stone. And in that time line, you die, Owen. Every single time, *you die*." She glared at him. "So tell me how to fix it! What advice do you have, huh? How do I keep my best friend from getting killed? And the worst part is, you always do it saving me! The circumstances change, but not the result."

"There's a way to fix this," Owen said, not entirely sure he was right. "There has to be."

"I thought that once," she said, turning away. "But now I know the truth. You can't fight destiny. I can't escape my fate, no matter what I do. Maybe the universe wants to be destroyed, so it keeps pushing me toward my fate until I go, willingly or not. Or maybe I'm just the ultimate evil and won't stop until I make everything go boom."

"Or maybe we just haven't found the right answer yet," he told her, forcing some optimism.

Kara shook her head. "Stop it. You sound just like you a year ago, when I first met you. But you already knew it was hopeless, because you found that out right now."

"I get it," Owen said quietly. "It's not easy, being out of control of your own story. Trust me. I know what it's like."

She grunted. "Another nonfictional thing, huh?"

"This one's more of a fictional thing, actually," he told her. "But it doesn't matter. We've all been at the mercy of other people at times. I mean, I've literally had someone choose what I could or couldn't do!"

"So how do you handle that?" she asked, and Owen could hear the anger rising in her voice.

He smiled without much humor. "Screaming and yelling, mostly. Hasn't worked so far, but I'm not giving up just yet."

"I tried yelling," Kara said, sitting back down across from him. "Asking whoever was listening what I did to deserve this. No one ever answered. Did you get any response?"

"Not the way you'd think," Owen said, "and it's not usually one I want to hear." He paused. "I think we have to tell ourselves that since we can't see all of the options, maybe what we're getting isn't so bad. Maybe there are far worse things out there that we're being protected from."

Kara snorted. "No way. This has got to be the darkest time

line. If anyone out there is deciding things, they must really hate us."

That *was* a possibility. If the readers listened to Nobody, they probably did hate him. But what if they didn't? What if after reading about him and Bethany, they actually did want to help, but just didn't have a lot of choices? This was Nobody's doing, after all, so who knew what he was allowing the readers to choose from?

Readers had gotten them out of the time prison, after all. And now Owen could travel between stories, too. Granted, a lot of terrible things had happened along the way, but it wasn't like the story was over or something. What if the readers really had been doing their best to help, and he'd just been blaming them this whole time for things that were out of their control?

If nothing else, there was an easy way to answer those questions.

"I have an idea," Owen said, standing back up. "I think I know how to restart the TSA."

Kara sighed. "And how exactly can we do that? No one knows who founded it except the Countess, apparently. But she had all of time to find the founder, and we're going to get tracked the moment we step back into my world. She'll capture us, and that'll be that. The only thing that'd protect us is if we found the *exact* time of the founding, since in that moment, reality wouldn't have been changed yet. But there's no way of knowing when or where that moment is!"

"True," Owen said. "Except I think I have a way to *cheat* a bit and find that moment."

"You can't cheat destiny," Kara said. "Have you listened to what I've been telling you?"

"Well then, let's make it work for us instead of against us," he said. "I'm going to ask for a favor. It might backfire, but I'm not sure what other choice we have. Besides, it can't hurt to be a bit optimistic for a change."

She seemed confused but slowly stood up and took his hand. "So what do you want me to do?"

"Just pick a place and time to travel to, whatever pops into your head," Owen said, hoping he was right about this. "But don't do it just yet. Wait until I bring us back into your world, and then the moment we hit, go for it."

Kara gave him an odd look but nodded. Owen closed his eyes and turned his thoughts outward.

Readers: I'm hoping I've been wrong about you all along, and if so, I'm really sorry. All I'm asking for is a sign. You've seen what we're up against, and as fictional people yourselves, I don't imagine you want us to leave Kara's reality under the control of the Countess. Not to mention whatever Nobody is going to do to your world when he separates it from the nonfictional one. So I hereby grant you the power to choose again. Please, help us! You have the power to fix things and save everyone. All you have to do is tell Kara where to send us.

He paused, crossing his fingers for this next part. *I know you don't know where the founder of the TSA is either . . . unless you know something I don't, I guess. But I know what these Pick the Plot books are like. You can* cheat. *All you have to do is hold this page and flip ahead to check the various options. If we get captured by the Countess, turn back right away to this page and try again. Once you find the right one, then go from there. Okay?*

Thank you.

Owen slowly opened his eyes. "Now, are you ready?" he asked Kara.

She nodded, reaching for her bracelet.

Owen ripped a page open through the worlds and back into Kara's story. "Go!" he shouted, and together, they jumped through.

Readers, there is actually no need to "cheat" as Owen suggests. The time and place were revealed by the Time Security Agency founder earlier in this very book. If you don't remember, then by all means, try out each option below. No one will judge you.

HAVE KARA TAKE THEM TO LIVERPOOL IN 2515.

Turn to page 79. ⬍❯

HAVE KARA TAKE THEM TO BRANSON IN THE YEAR 14.

Turn to page 222. ⬍❯

HAVE KARA TAKE THEM TO KYOTO IN THE YEAR 10,000.

Turn to page 168. ⬍❯

HAVE KARA TAKE THEM TO TALLAHASSEE IN THE YEAR 2000.

Turn to page 184. ⬍❯

**HAVE KARA TAKE THEM TO
SOMERSVILLE IN THE YEAR 2054.**

Turn to page 270. ⬍❯

**HAVE KARA TAKE THEM TO MUNICH IN
THE YEAR 4120.**

Turn to page 33. ⬍❯

*G*ET UP! YOU CAN'T STAY IN BED ANYMORE!

The thought hit Owen so hard that he immediately leaped out of bed, his eyes flying open. Where had *that* thought come from?! Right before it hit, he'd been telling himself everything was going to be okay and that he didn't need to get up.

Now that his eyes were open, he took a chance and looked around. Unfortunately, even with almost no light in the room he could tell that this was definitely *not* his bedroom. First of all, the walls were only like seven or eight feet apart, just wide enough for the bed to fit between length-wise. Second, and more important, his windows at home weren't made out of metal bars. That right there was a pretty big clue. Not to mention the whole roaring thing.

Owen stepped onto the mattress and grabbed the bars over

the window, trying to peer through. It was just as dark outside, with no moon as far as he could tell. But even the non-terrifying sounds didn't make any sense. The buzzing insects, for example, were so loud it was like someone had turned their volume up as high as it could go.

Another growl-scream came from just outside the window, and Owen gasped, pushing himself out of sight of the window as his heart raced again. Or maybe it hadn't slowed down yet?

"Why did I get out of bed for this?" he whispered to himself.

Quietly, he stepped down off of the bed and moved slowly to the other side of the room, where bars formed a fourth wall. He felt around until he found something that seemed like a door, then gently pulled on it, hoping it was unlocked.

Nope, no such luck. Great. Had Nobody just stuck him in a jail cell to rot, then? Was this where he was supposed to learn what it was like to be a fictional person? Even if an author *was* in control of a fictional person's life (which Owen still didn't believe), that didn't mean the fictional person was stuck in a cell for their whole life! At least not unless you were making a really annoying analogy.

Owen banged his head into the bars over and over, silently cursing Nobody, the Dark, and himself (mostly himself) for getting into this. "I'm not going to spend the rest of my life here, am I?" he whispered.

Suddenly, the lights clicked on in both the room and the hallway outside. The cell door that Owen was hanging on to opened, pulling him halfway into the hallway. He quickly leaped back inside, not sure what else was out there, as a strange voice spoke from various speakers in the ceiling.

"Good morning, prisoners. Welcome to the last day of your life!"

Turn to page 177. ◆❯

L iverpool in the year 2515," Kara said, grabbing Owen's hand and hitting the bracelet. They jumped forward in time, only to appear in the middle of nothing. Everything was blank, a white world absent of anything, just like the space between stories.

"Wait, what happened?" Kara said. "The time bracelet says we're in the correct year, but this can't be the same place."

What did this mean? The world was just . . . gone. Had Nobody split the fictional and nonfictional worlds, and this was the result?

"Something's *very* wrong," Kara said.

"It sure is," said a voice, and they whirled around to find Dolores with several robed guards. She immediately touched Owen and Kara on the neck, and they both collapsed to the ground.

The last thing Owen heard was Dolores's voice getting farther and farther away. "Bring them, but keep them asleep. The Countess doesn't want them to wake up before she disposes of them."

Readers, turn back now! This is the . . . the wrong . . .

And then everything went dark.

As Dolores's hand touched his chest, Owen desperately hoped the readers had fulfilled his request. Uncertain what else to do, he willed his entire body to just . . . *stop*, to completely freeze the entire thing in time. If Dolores could use his powers this way, then he could too, assuming the readers had agreed to it! And now even if Dolores stopped time around his heart, the rest of him would be frozen too, and no damage would be done. Then he'd be able to unfreeze all of himself later, and everything would be fine!

That was the theory, at least. Unfortunately, it didn't work.

As Dolores froze time around his heart, pain shot out through Owen's entire body, and he gasped. Dolores grinned at this, then stood up to get a better view as he grabbed for his chest, the world going dark all around him. What had happened?

Had the readers not heard him? They couldn't have just left him to die, could they?

Really, readers? That was just cruel. Why don't you put the book down for a while and think about what you've done. Then come back and try the other choice by turning to page 157.

IME FOR ACTION. CHOOSE A CHALLENGE AND GET OUT OF HERE ALREADY!

Yes! It was time to get things done! He almost leaped toward the nearest air lock before stopping himself. Where had that thought come from? Time for action? That's not something he'd ever say. What *was* this?

"Owen?" Kara said, and stepped closer.

"I'm fine," he told her, rubbing his temples. Why would he think something like that? It was almost like when he'd been writing thought bubbles for Bethany, and—

"Wait a second," Owen said, his eyes opening in just about every way. "No. Oh *no*."

This was a Pick the Plot book. That meant readers were choosing how the story progressed. But they weren't making decisions for Kara, the story's main character.

They were choosing *Owen's* adventure.

"Are you *kidding* me?" he whispered, looking all around the ceiling as if he could see the readers. But that didn't make sense, they wouldn't be visible. He tried thinking at them instead.

You're telling me what to do? That's what these loud thoughts have been? You ordering me to do stuff?

"You look like you've seen a ghost," Kara said to him. "What's going on?"

Owen gritted his teeth to keep himself from screaming. How was this fair? Random readers were deciding what happened to his life? No way. They weren't in control here, *he* was! He wasn't fictional, and they couldn't just change his story to whatever they wanted.

. . . Could they?

"It's . . . one of those nonfictional things," Owen told her, repeating what she'd said to him back when the Countess had attacked. "Sorry, I just have something to work through. It's probably better if you don't know."

She nodded, but he could tell she was worried about him. This whole Kara thing wasn't exactly helping his mood either, honestly. "Just let me know if I can do anything," she told him, and took a step back.

He bit his lip hard, then forced himself to smile. "All good," he told her. "Which air lock were you thinking?"

That's right, readers. I'm going to let her *pick. This is one choice you* don't get! *Try to tell me what to do again, and we'll see who's in control here.*

Kara pointed at the first one, labeled with a large "1" over the door and a simple-looking analog clock right below it. "Each air lock has a clock, and all three are running differently. I'm guessing that's a clue about the challenge."

She was right. The first clock was moving clockwise, but much faster than normal; the hands were practically flying around the face. The second one's hands froze in place for about a minute, then moved forward normally for five seconds, while the third was running at a normal pace but backward, counterclockwise.

"I'm happy to choose," she said. "But didn't you say something about a nonfictional way to remember the code? Maybe you should pick instead, if that's the case."

Owen dug his fingernails into his palms, trying not to say anything he shouldn't, at least not out loud. Finally, he took a deep breath. "You're probably right," he said. "Let me think about it for a second."

She smiled, and he closed his eyes.

Well, readers? You're all about telling me what to do, why don't you go ahead and pick? You're the ones who are going to have to remember this code and all. Go for it! Tell me how to live my own life. Because that's not messed up at all, not in any way. I hope you're happy with yourselves!

Let's see your amazing, genius pick, readers! Come on!

HAVE OWEN PICK AIR LOCK ONE.

Turn to page 260. ⬧⟩

HAVE OWEN PICK AIR LOCK TWO.

Turn to page 317. ⬧⟩

HAVE OWEN PICK AIR LOCK THREE.

Turn to page 110. ⬧⟩

**OWEN'S BEING A JERK. MAKE HIM
PUNCH HIMSELF IN THE FACE.**

Turn to page 366. ⬧⟩

YOU HAVE TO SEE THE DINOSAURS. GO LOOK OUT THE WINDOW!

The thought plowed through Owen's thoughts like a runaway train, and almost before he knew it he was standing on the bed's scratchy blanket with his face pushed as far through the bars as it could fit.

Outside, giant leafy plants blocked almost all view; it was the thickest jungle Owen had ever seen. He squinted his eyes, trying to make something out using the light from the room, but it was just too dark outside.

And then Owen realized that the insect noises had all grown quiet, and he could actually make out something between the leaves. A pair of green-and-yellow-flecked eyes, each at least three inches wide, stared back at him, then slowly blinked.

YIKES, OKAY, THAT'S ENOUGH. GET OWEN AWAY FROM THE WINDOW BEFORE HE'S EATEN.

Turn to page 278. ⬍❯

YAY, A DINOSAUR! HAVE OWEN REACH A HAND OUT TO PET IT!

Turn to page 182. ⬍❯

*R*UN! HIDE! NO ONE IN HERE SHOULD KNOW
WHO YOU ARE!

The thought hit Owen like a tidal wave, and before he could even think clearly, he was off, pushing past the girl.

"Sorry, you've got me confused with someone else," he said over his shoulder, moving quickly down the hall, not knowing why, just that he had to run, to hide, *to get away from her*. He slipped behind a large, round prisoner covered in tattoos of different digital times. How had she known his name? Was she working with Nobody? Maybe she was here to make sure he never escaped!

"Owen, I know it's you," the girl said, and he started moving again, sliding past a group of prisoners talking about which challenge to try first. He glanced back to see if she was following him and almost ran into another prisoner, who pushed him aside, growling.

There wasn't anywhere to actually hide in here, not in such close quarters. How could he get away from her? How could . . .

Wait. *Why* was he trying to hide again? She had asked what he was doing here, which meant she wasn't expecting to see him. That meant she probably wasn't working for Nobody. Anyone he'd sent would know Owen was there.

So what had sent him running like that? He'd just felt so fearful, so *paranoid* all of a sudden. But the more he thought about it, the less intense the feelings were, and with a deep breath, he was able to push them aside and turn around to face the girl.

"Um, hi?" Owen said as she strode toward him, looking far angrier than he'd have liked.

WAY TO GO, OWEN. YOU MESSED IT UP.

Turn to page 103. ⬍⟩

*T*ELL KARA THAT YOU'LL NEVER SEE HER AGAIN IF SHE GOES, AND YOU CAN'T TAKE THAT.

The thought exploded in his head, and his mouth opened before he could stop himself. "Kara, I'll never—"

He immediately clamped both hands over his mouth, turning bright red. What had he just been about to say? Had that been the readers?

What are you trying to do? he thought at them. *I just met her today! That doesn't help!*

"I would have just let the agent take me," Kara was saying, not looking at him. "But I had to make sure you got to the right time myself. Can't let you have adventures in time without me, you know?"

I need something else! Owen thought as loudly as he could. *Really, I'll take anything!*

**OWEN SHOULD SAY THAT LEAVING
WITH HIM TO ANOTHER STORY WOULD
FIX THINGS.**

Turn to page 8. ♦>

**OWEN SHOULD SAY THAT THEY'LL
FIND A WAY TO FIX THINGS IN THE
FUTURE.**

Turn to page 180. ♦>

The woman's staff glowed, and a shimmering light much like the one guarding the city appeared around Owen and Kara, growing over them like a bubble. Owen tried to push his hand through it, but his touch just sent tiny ripples out in every direction.

"I have a bad feeling about this," he told Kara.

"Isn't that one of those lines from *Star Fights*?" she said, putting her hands on the bubble as well, as if to feel for a weak spot. "I've heard you talk about those movies so much I feel like I've seen them."

Owen had no idea what to say to *that*, so he just slumped against the shimmering light. Fine. Magicians from the no-longer-lost city of Atlantis had captured them, and they couldn't escape. But there was still a bright side: At least these magic-users had to be better than facing the Magister, Kiel Gnomenfoot's teacher. After he'd found out his whole life existed in a book series, the Magister had gone insane and tried to kill not only Bethany, but Kiel and the author of the books, not to mention the entire science planet of Quanterium. Hopefully, if these magicians learned the same news, they'd handle it a *bit* better.

If this was even still the fictional world at all.

The bubble rose into the air, which made both Owen and Kara reach out to steady themselves, but the flight was remarkably smooth. They bobbled gently along behind the woman as she floated into the city. Back over the ocean, the magical wall sizzled constantly now, even collapsing in places as lightning bolts sent more magic-users falling to the sand or water.

As they passed over the city itself, people ran or floated in all directions both above and below them. Even though it looked like widespread panic, no one was making any sound, so the city stayed deathly quiet. Maybe they were speaking by magic? Or maybe they could see the future and knew this attack had been coming, so weren't surprised?

The rainbow buildings became more and more ornate as they floated through the city, now growing together like some sort of coral reef. It was all so beautiful and distracting that

Owen almost missed seeing a hundred-foot-tall statue step off its platform, then stride back toward the beach with earth-quaking steps.

Huh. Apparently the magic wall wasn't their only defense.

Behind them, Owen heard something explode, and he turned to see one of the buildings closest to the ocean covered in fire. Whoever was attacking must have gotten through the wall already. And now that he and Kara were trapped here, they'd probably be seen as enemies by the invaders, too. This whole thing just kept getting worse.

Their speed picked up, and soon they were floating through a large decorated archway and straight into a tower so tall he couldn't see the top. Owen gaped, wondering how it could possibly be real as he craned his neck to look up. No skyscraper in the real world was that large, not even close. And they'd built this with magic?

Inside, the tower was completely hollow, without even a stairway leading up. The interior walls were covered in elaborate designs and what looked like words, but in an alphabet Owen had never seen before. The words intertwined with the art seamlessly, and again, he had to look away to keep from losing himself in the beauty.

Their bubble quickly rose through the empty tower, its speed steadily increasing until the walls sped by so fast the art all blended together. Finally they slowed and passed through another shimmering light to land in the middle of what looked like a meeting chamber.

Twelve chairs made of light rose out of the shimmering substance that made up the floor, and in each one sat a human being that looked at least a few centuries old, if not more. The bubble surrounding Owen and Kara disappeared, but none of the elders said a word. Could these people even speak, let alone move? They looked so frail! Were these chairs the only thing holding them up?

One of the twelve, maybe the oldest—except they *all* looked like the oldest—turned to face Owen and Kara. "What have you brought us, Adelaine?" he said in a voice much stronger than he looked.

"Hope," she said, bowing. "Or so I believe, Magister."

Wait. *What*, now? Owen's spine turned to ice at the very mention of the name. But there was no way. That was just a coincidence, probably a term of respect or something! This incredibly old man looked nothing like Kiel's evil teacher, other than that they both had white hair and long beards, and were wearing magical-looking robes. But what male wizard didn't have all of those things?

Maybe she hadn't even *said* "magister" anyway! Who was to say that these magicians were speaking English? They probably had translator spells, and if that was the case, Owen's brain had probably just substituted the word "magister" for something else since he was used to it. That had to be it!

"There *is* no hope," another of the council members said, this one a woman so delicate that it looked as if her bones had abandoned her body. "We have foreseen that the Naturalists *will* destroy us. The future is written in stone and cannot change. We must flee if we are to survive."

"That is exactly the hope I bring," Adelaine said. "These two come from the *future*. Look at them closely, and tell me that you see what I do. I prayed that I hadn't gone mad when I first set eyes upon them!"

The council members each took up their staffs, books, or wands, and Owen felt his hair rise on end as twelve separate glows appeared around both him and Kara. Assorted gasps and murmurings filled the room, and Owen cringed.

Readers, this is so your fault. You and I both know that you could have fixed the time bracelet and jumped us back to the future at any point, and yet, here we are. *I hope you see what you've done. We're interfering with an entire universe, and for all we know, this might stop Kara's from ever existing! Are you okay with that?*

"But what proof do we have that these two come from the future?" asked a third council member.

"You can see it as easily as I, Estran," Adelaine said, and Owen frowned. Shouldn't she have called him "magister" too? Or shouldn't his brain have translated it that way? Maybe the previous "magister" had been a title, and this was a name. At least, he hoped that was the case. "Neither of these children could possibly have resulted from our world."

"Then we are in agreement," said the first man, the one Adelaine had called Magister. "The plan to build a new reality for ourselves and our children *must* move forward immediately. These two children are the surest sign yet that we have no other choice. But we must delay no further, or there will be no one left to save, and no magic remaining in *any* reality, let alone this one."

"But, Magister," said a fourth council person, "our magic will not be nearly enough to build an entire new universe. It's not possible!"

The first council member chuckled. "Has anything ever been

impossible with magic, Uthella? Though your question brings up a related point: Building a world on pure possibility will require a grounding, a foundational stability. For that reason, I submit that we will have to keep a connection open between our worlds, the old and new. Without it, I foresee our new reality falling to pieces."

"You worry about the new world, yet Uthella is right," Estran said. "Even with our entire city, we won't have the power to do this!"

"True," the first council member said. "But our magic is not the only source left in this world."

A few of the other council members gasped. "You can't mean . . . ," Estran said, then trailed off.

"I do indeed," the Magister said. "We must take, and *use*, the magic inborn in each Naturalist as well, and every other human being on this planet. Without it, we would not hope to have enough power."

Another round of murmuring filled the room, this time louder. "Monstrous!" shouted one of the council members. "We would become no better than they!"

"You would leave them with only their . . . science?" another council member asked, a disgusted look on her face.

"Societies would regress back thousands of years, if not more!" said another member. "We would be dooming them for millennia."

"Not if we leave them a connection, as I mentioned," the Magister said.

"What do you mean, Magister?" Adelaine asked.

"We need their natural magical power," the Magister said, looking from council member to council member. "But that doesn't mean we will leave them helpless. Just as we need their stability, they will need our possibility. I offer this plan: In place of the magic within their minds, we connect them to our new reality with a sort of 'third eye.' With this, they could witness everything they rejected, yes, but also have an entire realm of limitless opportunity at hand. Then they'd have all the power they'd need to survive, and thrive." He paused. "I realize that this connection would be as much a curse as a gift for those remaining. But maybe they'll use it to realize what they've done, and one day welcome us back so that we might all be whole once more."

The council chamber went silent as they seemed to ponder this.

"You've all seen proof that it can be done," the Magister

said, pointing at Owen. "Look again into the boy's mind if you must. He has no magic in him, yet within his mind there is still a connection to it. He can *see* infinite possibilities, even if he can't control them."

Owen's eyebrows shot up. He could see what, now? What was the magician talking about with infinite possibilities?

"But the girl is different," another member said.

"She is," the Magister said. "And I believe I know why. But that can wait."

"I'm not really following this," Kara whispered out the side of her mouth.

"I got lost back at the beach," Owen whispered back.

"Does the council hereby approve the plan, then?" the Magister said.

Each of the twelve nodded in turn, ending on the first member, who slowly stood up. Owen could hear his bones creaking, even from a distance. But then the man tapped his staff on the ground, and the years began to fall off of him like leaves from a tree.

And what remained was the same man Owen had met in the Kiel Gnomenfoot books, the Magister.

No. *No, no, no, no, no.* This wasn't possible! How could the

Magister be *here*? He wasn't a part of Kara's story! And besides that, this was beyond Kara's entire *reality*. How could this be, even in an impossible world?

The sounds of explosions grew closer, and the entire building began to sway. The council members looked at each other nervously, and Adelaine took Owen and Kara's hands. "You have given us hope, children," she said. "In payment, perhaps we can aid you in your return to your proper time."

"Hold, Adelaine," the Magister said, and walked over to Owen with confident, strong strides. He bent down and peered closely into Owen's eyes. "No, these two will remain with us. I am not yet finished with them. Bring them along."

. . . Uh-oh.

Turn to page 18. ⬍>

W hy did you come here?" the pink-haired girl asked, moving closer to Owen, her eyebrows furrowed. "I told you in my note I didn't want you following me. I *chose* this."

Note? Owen's mouth moved, but no words came out. "Guh?" he said.

She shook her head, then stepped forward and surprised Owen by hugging him tightly. "It's so good to see you," she whispered, her voice a bit shaky. "But you *really* shouldn't have come."

Okay, what was going on? First she knew his name, then she claimed to have left him a note, and now it was good to see him? Who *was* this girl? Had he somehow taken the place of a character in the book also named Owen? That'd be a huge coincidence, but Nobody could have made it happen. Except the name on his jumpsuit was Smith, and—

The girl pulled away from him, looking annoyed again. "But why did you come? I'm not leaving, I don't care what you say."

Owen nodded, trying to figure out why exactly this other Owen might have dropped into the prison. "Oh, I know you won't be convinced," he said carefully. "But, um . . . I had to check, just to be sure." Right, that sounded good! "But now that I have, I should get out of here, go back home or something. I'll leave you to your life in prison and keep your note as a reminder not to bother you again."

Totally convincing, if Owen did say so himself.

The girl just stared at him for a moment. "You have no idea who I am, do you?"

Or maybe not. Owen tried to look shocked. "What are you talking about? Of *course* I know you. I told you, I came here to, um . . ."

She raised a questioning eyebrow but seemed to be having trouble not smiling. "Oh yeah? *Then what's my name?*"

"Okay, you got me," Owen said, dropping his head in defeat. He closed his eyes, bracing for anger, shock, or even disbelief from whoever this was.

"That explains so much," the girl said, and Owen opened his

eyes to find her staring up at him with worry. "Did Nobody send you here? Is this when we meet for the first time?"

She knew about Nobody? And what did she mean, for the first time? "Where we . . . meet?"

The girl nodded. "This *is* the first time, it must be. Or at least the first time *you* meet *me*. You wouldn't ever tell me about it, because you didn't want me to know about my future." She paused, looking away for a second. "Well, *more* about it, anyway. Why didn't you tell me that was going to happen here, in the prison? Is that why you let me turn myself in, because you knew you'd be here . . . ?" She trailed off, then shook her head. "What am I thinking? None of that matters right now. If Nobody left you here, we have to get you out, and fast."

"How do you know that name?" Owen asked, his mind struggling to catch up to whatever was happening here. Now she knew about Nobody, and this wasn't the first time she had met Owen? Except it was the first time Owen met her?

Was this all a time travel thing? Because if so, *this* was why time travel never made sense. How could he have met her at a different time than she met him? Even trying to get it straight in his head confused him.

"Try not to think about it," the girl said, grabbing his hand and leading him down the hall. "If Nobody did put you here, then I'm going to get you out again. You heard the voice: We need a three-digit code to open the exit door, so that's what we're going to do." She stopped them both suddenly. "Hey, don't tell anyone my real name here, okay? If any of the criminals knew who I *really* was, they could go back and prevent me from ever being born. And trust me, there's already a line of people waiting for that chance."

"I don't *know* your real name," Owen said, fighting through the confusion. "Or your fake name. What should I call you?"

She grinned a bit in embarrassment. "Ugh, right, I forgot. From my perspective, I've known you for almost a year at this point. It's so odd that you don't remember any of it. Except it's not memory for you because it hasn't happened yet." She nodded almost to herself. "Well, just call me Kara while we're here, okay?"

Kara? That sounded familiar somehow. Wasn't there a time travel book series about a girl named Kara something? Kara . . .

"Dox?" Owen asked. "Kara Dox?"

Her eyes lit up. "You do know—" But she stopped in mid-sentence, her face falling again. "No, you just recognize the name from the books. I remember." She sighed deeply. "Doesn't matter. Just follow my lead in here, and I'll keep you safe, okay? After all, you helped me during that time when—" She stopped and rolled her eyes. "Wow, I can't stop giving everything away. C'mon." She grabbed Owen's hand and pulled him toward the end of the hallway again.

Kara Dox. Why couldn't he remember anything else about the series? He'd seen it randomly, but couldn't even remember the cover, let alone the plot. Why had Nobody chosen this story? And this couldn't be the first book in the series, either. So why this one? Just because it was about a prison?

And given that this was a prison, a question occurred to him: Why was *Kara* here? She seemed nice enough, but for all Owen knew, she could be the villain of the series.

"Before we go out there," Owen said, dragging her to a stop, "maybe I should learn a bit more about you."

She gave him a curious look, then seemed to get what he meant. "Oh, right," she said, looking away. "You want to know why I'm here, in time prison. That's fair."

"I'm sure you're great and all, I just want to make sure you didn't break a time code that involved murdering people or something." He smiled, hoping to make it a joke, but stopped when she didn't grin in return.

"I belong here, Owen," she said quietly, staring at the floor. "Right now, that's . . . that's all you really need to know. I turned myself in voluntarily, and won't be leaving no matter what. This is where I need to be, for the safety of . . . everyone."

"Oh, Ms. Dox," said a low, growly sort of voice from around a corner. "You two won't be safe in here. Not while *I'm* locked in here with you."

Kara instantly shoved Owen back against the wall behind her, then moved in front of him protectively. "Who's there?" she asked, fists held up in front of her.

A woman with bright white hair and an elaborate gray cloak wrapped around her shoulders stepped into the hallway. As far as Owen had seen, she was the only one in the prison not wearing an orange jumpsuit.

"Just me, my dear," she said, giving them both a hungry smile. "It's been too long since I've seen you and your little friend there. How lovely. As I was saying, considering *you* are the one who ruined my plans and handed me over to the

Time Security agents, I'm afraid I have to disagree with you protecting anyone." She slowly pulled a long, silky glove onto her right hand, and it began to glow. "Now, tell me, Ms. Dox: How do you wish to die?"

WHOA. HAVE OWEN ATTACK THE STRANGE WOMAN BEFORE SHE CAN TOUCH THEM WITH THAT GLOVE.

Turn to page 250.

THAT'S TOO DANGEROUS. HAVE OWEN KEEP AWAY FROM THAT GLOWING GLOVE.

Turn to page 349.

AIR LOCK THREE.

The thought banged around in Owen's head so hard it echoed. That had to have been on purpose. He winced at the pain but kept his thoughts under control as best he could. *Don't blame the readers. This is* Nobody's *fault.*

Besides, if this was the only way to save Bethany, then he didn't really have any choice but to listen to them, did he? Assuming the readers hadn't decided *that* for him too.

"Let's do the third one," he told Kara, pointing at the clock moving backward. They walked over to where a small group of prisoners already stood milling around, no one quite sure what to do.

"If we go in, who's to say we come out?" asked a woman with an eye patch, talking to a human-shaped robot made from some sort of bronze-colored metal. "I think these air locks are all traps. That's exactly the kind of game the Time Security Agency would play with us."

"INDEED," said the robot. "THIS PLACE WAS CREATED TO KEEP ME SAFE, YET IMPRISONED. LOGICALLY, THEREFORE, THEY WOULD NOT ALLOW ANYONE TO ESCAPE, CERTAINLY NOT AFTER HAVING FOUND OUT THAT THE TSA'S CREATOR RESIDES WITHIN. STILL, THERE IS A POSSIBILITY THAT THE DESIGNERS LEFT WEAKNESSES WITHOUT REALIZING THEY DID SO. I'D SUGGEST WE CONTINUE WITH THE CHALLENGE AND FIND OUT."

Kara's eyes widened. "Wait, that robot founded the TSA?" she whispered to Owen. "If that's true, why would it ever admit that in a room full of criminals that the TSA jailed?"

"You built all of this?" an enormous prisoner said to the robot, towering over it. "You're saying I'm in here because of you?"

"I DID NOT SPECIFY ANY SUCH THING," the robot responded. "AND I DID NOT BUILD THIS TIME PRISON. I AM JAILED HERE, JUST AS YOU ARE."

"Maybe without you, the TSA won't exist," the prisoner said, and grinned widely. Several of his teeth had been replaced with what looked like holograms. "Why don't we find out?" He swung an enormous meaty fist right at the robot's chest.

The robot's hand flashed out faster than Owen could even see and stopped the punch in midair. The prisoner gasped in pain, then began whimpering as the robot picked the man up by his fist. "I WOULD NOT RECOMMEND ANY OTHERS TRY SUCH A THING," it said to the other prisoners grouped around, then proceeded to bang the prisoner against the floor over and over before dropping his unconscious body. "ALSO, IT SHOULD GO WITHOUT SAYING THAT MY EXISTENCE, IF DELETED, WOULD BE REBOOTED AS OF MIDNIGHT TONIGHT. NOTHING YOU DO WITHIN THESE WALLS WOULD AFFECT THE OUTSIDE TIME LINE."

The woman with the eye patch nodded. "Anyway, if you think we should try, I'm willing to. It's not like we have much choice." She and the robot moved toward the door as Kara gave Owen a "what just happened?" sort of look.

"Why would they lock their founder in their own prison?" Owen asked.

"Remember what I said about time travelers going back to keep you from being born?" she said, watching the robot examine the air lock. "Well, everyone in here would probably stop the TSA from being founded if they could. The founder's identity is the agency's most protected secret." She wrinkled her nose. "If they did build this place just to keep him protected, it seems like a pretty awful way to treat your founder."

Yikes. This TSA didn't play around. Neither did prisoners like the Countess, though. Owen glanced back at the ones who'd chosen to stay behind and just enjoy the food and entertainment. When this was all over, hopefully those prisoners wouldn't turn out to be the smart ones.

"See, I told you to eat," Kara said, bumping him again with her shoulder. "Look at you, you're practically drooling. Never miss breakfast, Owen. Most important meal of the day, I hear."

The eye-patch woman and the robot opened the air lock together, and Kara grabbed Owen by the hand and led him in. A few other prisoners pushed their way in too.

Inside looked like every air lock Owen had ever seen in a science-fiction movie: basically a short room with large doors on either end, each one locked with a wheel. As soon as they were all inside, the door abruptly closed behind them and red lights began flashing as a siren rang out in short bursts, like an alarm clock.

The robot approached the door they'd just gone through, and tried reopening it. "IT APPEARS WE ARE LOCKED IN," it said. "YOU HAVE INDEED PREDICTED OUR SITUATION CORRECTLY, MS. TANNER."

The woman with the eye patch cringed. "Please don't use my name, TIME-R. I doubt the rest of these people have the same ethical programming as you do, and they wouldn't hesitate to delete both of us from time."

"MANY HAVE TRIED TO DELETE ME FROM TIME," TIME-R said, moving slowly in a circle and staring at each of them in turn. "NONE OF THEM STILL EXIST."

"I think we should have picked a different challenge," Owen whispered to Kara, who was staring intently at the opposite air lock door.

"I don't know," she told him. "I have a feeling this one will be the easiest. Remember how the clock outside went backward? I bet that's a clue. Maybe we'll have to walk backward the entire time, or even *speak* backward." She concentrated. "Newo. Newo. Your name is pretty easy backward, actually. Mine would be Arak, which sounds a bit like a dinosaur." Her eyes widened. "I wonder if there'll *be* any dinosaurs outside the air lock? We *are* in the Cretaceous

114

period, after all, and I've never seen one. Seems like as good a time as any."

"DINOSAURS ARE THE MOST EFFICIENT KILLERS IN RECORDED TIME," TIME-R told her. "I WOULD HAVE SUPPOSED THAT A HUMAN BEING MIGHT NOT WANT TO MEET SUCH A CREATURE, AS SHE WOULD SURELY BE EATEN BY IT."

"Maybe it'll eat the robot first," Kara whispered to Owen. "As long as there are dinosaurs, I'll be happy."

The lights and alarm stopped, and the opposite door opened. Before any of them could move, though, an enormous flash of light flooded over them, so bright it was physically painful. Owen shouted out in surprise, covering his eyes with his arm, only for the light to immediately disappear.

"What was that?" he said, giant spots of light taking up all of his vision.

"I'm not sure," Kara said from his side, "but I was wrong. Even if there are dinosaurs, I'm not happy."

The spots faded from Owen's eyes just enough for him to make out the scene around them.

They were no longer in the air lock. All of the other prisoners had also disappeared.

And now they were standing on top of a volcano, with lava rapidly flowing up the mountain *toward* them.

"Well," Owen said. "Can't say I saw that coming."

UH, WHAT? FIND OUT WHAT HAPPENED.

Turn to page 35. ⬦❯

THIS MUST BE A HALLUCINATION OR SOMETHING. JUMP INTO THE LAVA!

Turn to page 65. ⬦❯

"Watch out!" Kara shouted, and yanked Owen out of the way of the dinosaur. Enormous teeth clamped shut where he'd just been standing, and the massive creature reared back in anger, then roared.

"AHH!" Owen shouted. Having no idea what else to do, he did the exact opposite of every instinct and ran straight at the monster, Kara yanked along behind him. They ran for the monster's legs, ducking beneath a much-too-close bite.

The monster growled low and angry, twisting around to reach them, but they kept themselves as low to the ground as they could, right beneath the Tyrannosaurus rex's stomach.

"I don't know that this is a good long-term plan!" Kara shouted as the beast snapped its jaws shut just out of reach.

"At least he can't eat us down here!" Owen said, then

flattened back against her as a six-inch-long claw came slicing at his midsection.

Whoops! How could he forget that the T. rex's mouth wasn't the dinosaur's only weapon? Each of three toes per foot contained one of those massive claws, and that was six too many for Owen's comfort right now. And there wasn't a way to escape from the creature's feet, not while staying safe from its horrendous teeth.

"This way!" Kara shouted, and pulled Owen out of another swipe of the creature's talons, then straight toward the monster's tail. Though it thrashed around, they managed to make it safely out from beneath the T. rex. For a moment Owen almost sighed in relief. If they could keep behind it, then they'd be safe from both teeth *and* claws!

The tail swung out, plowing straight into both of them. The force of the blow sent them flying, and everything around Owen tumbled precariously until he slammed into leaves as tall as he was, breaking his fall. He hit the ground hard, and for a moment couldn't breathe. That panicked him, but what truly terrified him was the knowledge that he'd lost hold of Kara.

Wherever she was right now, her personal time was moving so slowly, she'd be completely frozen to the T. rex.

Not waiting to catch his breath, Owen pushed himself to his feet. Back on the path, he heard the monster roar, then come rumbling in his direction, so Owen froze, hiding behind the same leaves that had cushioned his fall. A T. rex could only make out movement, right? That was one of those points they'd made in the *Jurassic Park* movie. So if he just stayed still, everything should be okay.

Assuming the movie had any idea what it was talking about.

Beyond the leaves, Owen heard the creature stop just a few feet away. Enormous snorting almost like sniffing erupted out of sight, drawing closer and closer as he began sweating from the terror and the humidity both.

The leaf just in front of him pushed forward, and Owen's eyes widened as he leaned back as far as he could without actually taking a step. The leaf trembled with the T. rex's sniffing, and Owen held his breath, just in case it gave him away.

Then finally, after what felt like hours, the leaf fell back into place, and he heard the creature move on down the path. Owen's legs began to buckle from relief, but the thought of where the dinosaur might be headed kept him upright.

Kara. Where had she landed? Wherever it was, she'd be

motionless, so that might help save her, right? Except the dinosaur hunter had been frozen too, relative to how fast the T. rex was moving, and that hadn't helped the poor man. Should he chance it and try to find her quickly? Or was it smarter to wait for the T. rex to get farther away?

Don't even try to make this choice for me, Owen thought at the readers, then set off as quietly as he could, his robotic heart racing from worry.

Though the jungle kept him hidden, it also made getting anywhere take a lot longer, so Owen made his way back to the path that led away from the air lock, where they'd run from the T. rex. Back in the air lock, he could just make out the other prisoners, all basically frozen in time. But where was Kara? He'd been thrown a good ten feet himself, so she should be somewhere around too . . .

And then he saw something bright pink sticking out of some leaves a few feet past where he'd emerged, and his whole body went cold. He ran over to her, not caring about the noise he made anymore, just repeating over and over to himself, *Please don't be dead. Please don't be dead.*

He plowed through the plants next to her and dropped to her side, letting out a huge breath when he saw that she was at least still in one piece. She wasn't breathing, but then she *wouldn't* be, not with time moving as slowly as it was for her. He reached his hand out to touch her, then paused as he realized all the insects had stopped their buzzing.

Just in front of him, something chirped.

Owen looked up to find two green lizard-like eyes staring at him from between the leaves, just past Kara. And then something chirped behind him as well.

Owen slowly stood up, then glanced behind him, where another pair of eyes stared back. Whatever these things were, they were hunting him.

As the two dinosaurs watched him, Owen realized he really only had two options: 1) Let the creatures eat him first, then eat Kara; or 2) unfreeze Kara first, so they could be eaten together. At least the second way he wouldn't be alone for the next few seconds.

"I'm just going to help her up, okay?" he said slowly to the two dinosaurs still hidden in the leaves. "You do what you have to do, but she should be unfrozen for this. And hopefully she has more ideas than I do."

The creature nearest to Kara tilted its head and watched as Owen bent back down, taking Kara's hand in his. She groaned in pain and started to push to her feet. "Did something hit us?" she asked as Owen helped her up.

"Yes," he said carefully, looking between the two dinosaurs. "But more important, we're about to be eaten by raptors or something. Apparently whoever designed this place has only watched *Jurassic Park*." He raised his voice in frustration. "There are a lot more *herbivore* dinosaurs you could have put in here, you know! This is just clichéd!"

Kara quickly moved to stand in front of Owen, then circled around, one hand out in a calming gesture. "I think we might be okay," she said finally, and as she did, the two pairs of eyes disappeared into the leaves.

Owen blinked in surprise, not sure how they'd just been handed their lives back so suddenly. How had she done that? "Did you scare them off?"

Kara frowned. "Not me. Feel that?"

And then he did. The ground trembled over and over like something heavy was running toward them.

"Time to move!" Kara shouted, and yanked Owen back out to the trail as the T. rex exploded out of the nearby jungle, just ten or twenty yards away.

They ran as quickly as they could, though holding hands made it harder. Behind them the enormous monster quickly cut their lead in half, but even worse, Owen could hear the smaller possible velociraptors off to their right, matching their pace easily through the jungle. One of them turned its eerily stable head toward them in midrun, paused for a moment, then leaped straight at them.

"Duck!" Owen shouted, and yanked Kara to the ground. They slammed into the dirt path as the creature passed right over them, crashing into the woods on the other side of the path.

"C'mon!" Kara shouted, leaping up and pulling Owen to his feet. Behind them the T. rex was barreling closer, letting out earth-shaking roars. Kara began to run and Owen moved to follow, only to fall back to the ground as something grabbed his shoe, and he lost Kara's grip as he tumbled.

He twisted around and kicked over and over with his other foot, not even looking, until he heard something shriek as his shoe connected with what Owen hoped was a dinosaur face, and suddenly he was free. He chanced a quick glance behind him as he stood up, hoping he'd hit something vulnerable on the creature.

A raptor lay on the ground, chirping in pain from Owen's kick. But the creature seemed to shake it off quickly and jumped to its feet just in time for the T. rex to snatch it up off the path in its enormous jaws.

"Go!" Owen shouted, pulling Kara into a dead run. The sound of another raptor joining the fight behind them gave Owen even more energy, and he barely took a breath as they plowed into the jungle. How big *was* this place? It seemed to go on and on for miles! Whatever the case, they needed a place to hide, and right now.

But where? There were plenty of trees to climb, but he doubted they could get high enough to stay out of the reach of the Tyrannosaurus. And anything on the ground would be serving them up on a plate for the raptors.

There was no way any of the prisoners could have ever won their way through this. Even at a relative equal speed, Owen was pretty sure they were going to be eaten. How could anyone without time powers even get this far?

Though if that was true, then this whole thing was a setup, and the time prison never really intended for its prisoners to leave. In that case, these obstacles were probably created to keep them from actually focusing on ways to break out. And considering there was no way to warn himself and the other prisoners the next morning, when this all started again, they were doomed to repeat it over and over.

A roar behind him yanked Owen out of his thoughts, and

he pulled Kara into the jungle, just before the path ended in a ravine.

"We need to hide," he gasped, trying to catch his breath. "Somewhere to wait until midnight. Don't care about the code. Just don't want to be eaten!"

Kara shook her head. "No deal. We came this far, and we have to get you out of the prison. You're going to get the code."

"Oh, *really*?" Owen said. "I'd love to hear how that's going to happen!"

She half smiled. "Don't worry. I've got a plan."

HAVE KARA SUGGEST THAT THEY CROSS THE RAVINE JUST AHEAD.

Turn to page 214.◆❯

HAVE KARA SUGGEST THAT SHE DISTRACT THE T. REX WHILE OWEN FINDS THE CODE.

Turn to page 41.◆❯

The bald woman touched Kara's neck, and Kara crumpled to the ground unconscious.

"No!" Owen shouted, grabbing for Kara too late. He turned on the woman behind him, not sure how to fight her, but knowing he wanted to, very, *very* badly.

"I wouldn't," the bald woman said, keeping her fingers between her and Owen. "One touch and you'll join your friend."

"Why would you do that?" Owen demanded. "We didn't get in your way!"

The woman shrugged. "True. But you're the only other ones brave enough to leave the air lock, and I need some help. Now, one of you I can keep an eye on, but two of you gets complicated. So you're going to do what I say, and maybe both you and your friend live to see midnight. If not, I knock you out too, and you're both dinosaur food."

126

Owen clenched his fists so hard he dug his nails into his palms. Why were people always using his friends against him? *Take a look at this, readers. This is exactly what Nobody tried to do to me, too, when he wanted me to betray Bethany! When I refused, he threw me in here. Think about who you're helping here.*

"Fine," Owen said out loud. "What do you want me to do? I thought you were looking for the code."

"I am," the bald woman said, throwing a quick glance over his shoulder. "This might look like the outdoors, but it's not. The jungle doesn't go much farther, in fact. We're pretty penned in here with that monster. But just a few more yards down the path I found a clue about the exit code. 'To find the code, you'll have to swallow your pride.'" She rolled her eyes. "So easy it's insulting. The code's going to be somewhere *inside* the T. rex."

Of all the things Owen expected her to say, that wouldn't have made the top thousand. "Inside the what, now?"

"My guess is, the code would have to be on the back of the dinosaur's throat," the woman said. "It'd have to be far enough in that you couldn't see it from outside the mouth, but I can't imagine they'd go so far as to put it in the stomach lining. No one's making it out from that far in." She paused, considering. "Maybe the uvula?"

Owen blinked at this, not sure how to process any of it. "What's a uvula?"

Time kicked in, and insects began buzzing all around them. Thirty or so yards away, the T. rex stomped back toward the air lock. The bald woman gave Owen a threatening look while putting her finger to her lips, telling him to stay quiet. Finally, time froze again, and she spoke.

"It's the thing that hangs down behind your tongue," the woman said, wiggling her finger. "It'll be one of those places for certain."

"Do dinosaurs even have those? I thought it was just humans and probably some monkeys. Besides, to see it . . . we'd need to get eaten."

"We need to get inside its mouth."

". . . Which usually involves being *eaten*."

"I seriously doubt we can pull apart the creature's jaws to see inside during the frozen time period," the woman said, "so we're going to have to time this very carefully." She shook her head. "The really annoying thing is, if I'd just run out and jumped into the dinosaur's mouth at the very start of this, I'd have the code already and could give it to the Countess."

"Do you even know who she is?" Owen asked.

"Of course," the bald woman said, glaring at him. "I'm her daughter."

Her . . . what, now?

"Her what, now?" Owen asked.

"I had to turn myself in to the TSA just to get in here," she said, giving him a cold, dead-eyed look. "If my mother doesn't escape, then she'll never have me, and I'll disappear from all of time. Trust me when I say, I'm not going to let that happen."

Owen sighed deeply. "So let me guess. You want me to be bait."

The woman half smiled at him. "Now you get it. But you'll have to follow my instructions *exactly*. If it bites into you, I'm not going to be able to get around your body to find the code in the time I have."

"Also, I'd be *eaten*!" Owen shouted.

"You'd be fine come morning," she said with a shrug. "Now come on, unless you want your friend to be the bait instead."

Owen gritted his teeth but followed her out into the path back to the starting point.

The air lock came into sight right as time restarted, so the woman had them hide in the jungle to the side of the path until it refroze again. The nearby T. rex seemed to have given up on them and gone back for easier prey in the air lock, though it still couldn't bypass the barrier to reach the prisoners inside.

After time stopped again, Owen could see a few of the prisoners gawking at the dinosaur. None of them stepped even a foot outside the air lock.

"It moves about ten feet per second, I'd estimate," the woman told Owen, pushing him out onto the path. "So you need to stand around, say, forty-five feet from it or so."

"I don't know about your math," Owen said, walking slowly toward the monster. Not to mention that he had no idea what forty-five feet even looked like. His whole body shook as he moved closer, and a little voice in his head screamed at him to run, flee, get away from this thing. But knowing Kara was back in the woods unconscious, he forced himself to keep moving. Finally, what he guessed was around fifty feet away (*not* forty-five, because that was way too close), he stopped.

"Now *don't move*," the bald woman said from the jungle just to his side. "If it has to chase you, this isn't going to work. But remember, don't let it close its jaws around you either."

"Oh, *okay*, I'll try to keep that in mind!" Owen shouted at her.

"Here it comes," the bald woman said, melting back into the jungle as time clicked on again.

Five. The T. rex turned and spotted Owen. It roared loudly, then started stomping toward him, its eyes focused on his.

Four. Owen's legs shook so hard he could barely keep his feet, but he hugged his arms around his body and gritted his teeth, willing himself as hard as he could not to move.

Three. The creature's footsteps shook the ground beneath him, and fear almost made Owen's brain shut down, but a little part of him still felt hope. The creature was still so far away . . .

Two. Just one more second. He might actually survive this after all!

And then the dinosaur lunged forward, its enormous jaws wide open—

THE T. REX EATS OWEN.

Turn to page 357. ◆〉

THE T. REX FREEZES WITH ITS MOUTH OPEN RIGHT IN FRONT OF OWEN.

Turn to page 170. ◆〉

*T*IME TO GET OUT OF HERE. GO TO THE EXIT DOOR.

The thought hit Owen like an earthquake in his brain, and he stumbled a bit. *What? You have the code already? But I just got here!* Not that he was complaining or anything. The sooner he got out of this place and got back to Jupiter City to rescue Bethany, the better. But still, it seemed like he'd skipped a bunch of steps.

Unless . . . was this not actually his first day in the prison? And if not, how many times had he been through this? If the readers already had the code, did that mean he'd actually finished all three challenges? And somehow survived?

Or even worse, what if he *hadn't* survived each time?

He rubbed his arms and legs, just to make sure they were real and hopefully had never been in a dinosaur's stomach. There was no way of knowing what might have happened during those lost days, so it was probably better not to think about it. And hey, maybe the readers just cheated and flipped through the book until they found the exit code. If that was the case, then this really could be his first day here! . . . Right?

"I, um, think we should just try the exit door," Owen told Kara.

She looked surprised. "You've already got the code? How did you do it?"

You better *have the code, readers! Or this is going to be really, really embarrassing.*

"Oh, you know, I've got my nonfictional ways," he said, forcing a smile.

She half smiled and hugged him tightly. "I knew you'd find it. But I didn't think even you could make it happen so quickly!"

Even him? She was acting like he wasn't someone who messed up all the time. That right there was proof that she couldn't know him very well.

She paused, then looked up at him. "I thought we'd have more time to hang out, too," she said quietly. "I didn't realize it'd be over so soon."

Owen turned bright red and patted her on the back. "Me

either. So I'm not sure how we're going to convince the Countess that we have the code. Any ideas?"

Kara stepped back, looking thoughtfully at the exit door. "How fast do you think you can input the code?"

Owen frowned. Right. He still didn't actually *have* the numbers. *Readers? Can you tell me the code now? That might help me get out faster.*

He waited, counting to thirty, but there was no response. *Great.* Huge *help. Not only are you trying to control me, but when I actually could use your assistance, you're nowhere to be found. I hate all of you.*

"It might take a minute," he said finally.

Kara nodded, then grabbed both of his shoulders, staring into his eyes intently like a coach before a big game. "Okay. *I'll get you that minute.* But you have to promise me that as soon as the door opens, you go through, then close and lock it, no matter what. Do you promise?"

He stared back nervously, not sure what she was implying. Of course he knew she'd turned herself in to the Time Security Agency to be put in the Jules Verne Memorial Time Prison. But how could she not leave if she had the chance? She'd be trapped here forever, locked up with the worst time criminals in all of history. She couldn't just stay behind. It didn't make any sense!

"I'm not helping you if you don't promise," Kara said, narrowing her eyes. "This is the only way it's going to work. Get yourself to the door, and I'll do the rest, but only if you leave immediately. *Do you promise?*"

He wanted to say no, that he wasn't going to just abandon her here. That this place might have good food and comfy couches, but this wasn't life, and whatever she thought she'd done (or was *going* to do), she didn't deserve *this*, no matter what.

But if he didn't go, then Nobody would find Bethany, and both the fictional and nonfictional worlds would suffer.

"I promise," he said finally, hating himself for it.

Kara smiled sadly, then hugged him close again. "It was so good to see you, Owen. Even for just a few minutes. Hopefully we had fun getting the codes. It'd be nice to remember, but that's okay, I have plenty of memories of you already."

Owen frowned but hugged her back, letting go as he saw other prisoners giving them a strange look. Kara nodded, then pushed him on his shoulder. "Get moving."

Owen obediently began walking in a purposefully casual manner toward the exit door. Out of the corner of his eye he caught the Countess watching him closely from where she guarded the door, but he made sure not to look directly at her in any way.

When he was about ten feet away, the Countess moved to block his path. Apparently his casual act hadn't been believable enough. "And what exactly are you doing?" she asked, raising her gloved hand into the air as it began to glow.

"Hey, old woman!" Kara shouted from a few yards away on the other side of the Countess. "I think we're all bored with you telling us what to do. Why don't *you* go find the exit code while the rest of us sit around here?"

The Countess's face turned several different colors at once, and she hissed like a snake. "You dare address me in such a manner? Paradox or not, I will destroy you, girl!"

"As if you *could*," Kara said, stepping on top of a table and putting her hands on her hips. "Do you know who I am? Do *all of you* know who I am?!" Several of the prisoners began to murmur among themselves, but Kara didn't give them a chance to respond. "I'm *Kara Dox*, and old lady, I eat people like you for breakfast. It's the most important meal of the day, you know."

At the mention of her name, several of the prisoners stepped back nervously, mumbling even louder.

"That can't be her, can it?"

"She's so *young*."

"But what if it *is* her? Have you heard what she's going to do?"

Owen paused midsneak toward the exit door, his curiosity about Kara winning out. What had all of the prisoners heard that he hadn't?

But no, this was Kara's distraction, and she was giving him time to escape. He couldn't waste that, no matter how much he wanted to know her future. As Kara kept shouting at the Countess, Owen slowly resumed his sneaking toward the door.

"I've ended civilizations and restarted extinct species," Kara continued, pacing along the table, hands still on her hips as she kicked various food items off. "I've eaten spiders just to prove I *could*." (Someone murmured, "Uh, *gross*?") "I've seen the dawn of creation and the end of the universe. I'm the worst time criminal that will ever exist, and if I get out, I'm going to destroy all of time and space. Now that we know who I am, let's just ask: Who do you think *you* are, Countess?"

The Countess looked like she was about to explode. "Who am *I*, child? The world quakes at my—"

"I actually already did the whole 'I'm awesome, here's who

I am' speech," Kara said, interrupting. "Maybe try something different?

"I'm the Countess of Sirius VIII," the white-haired woman shouted as a bald woman moved to stand behind her. "I've killed more Time Security agents than will ever exist. I've—"

"No you haven't," Kara said.

The Countess stopped. "Yes I have."

"Physically impossible. Stop lying."

Prisoners around them began to gasp. "The Time Security Agency lives in fear that I'll escape," the Countess shouted. "In all probability, I have already destroyed this prison to rescue myself!"

"In all probability, you need a shower," Kara said, holding her nose.

"You will show me *respect*!" the Countess shouted.

"Not in all probability!" Kara shouted back.

What was she doing? Even as a distraction, this was going too far! Owen took another step, his eyes on Kara, and bumped into something. He immediately jumped backward, ready to fight, but it turned out he'd run into the exit door. Whoops! At least he'd made it.

"I will destroy you for all of *time*," the Countess said, her voice low and dangerous. She held up her glowing glove, then turned to the rest of the prisoners. "Bring her to me! The first of you who does will be granted a place beside me at my court once we're free!"

Uh-oh. Turning from the door, Owen watched as prisoners advanced on Kara, led by the bald woman, whoever she was. He couldn't just let her be turned into dust by the Countess, no matter how close to escaping he was. He had to help!

But if he didn't leave now . . . he might never get another chance. And then what would happen to Bethany? Not to mention both the fictional and nonfictional worlds themselves, if Nobody permanently separated them!

OWEN SHOULD HELP KARA.

Turn to page 188. ⬩❯

OWEN MADE A PROMISE. HE SHOULD PUT THE CODE INTO THE EXIT DOOR AND GET OUT. TO GIVE OWEN THAT CODE, TURN TO THE PAGE NUMBER THAT MATCHES THE CODE YOU'VE FOUND. (IF YOU HAVE PROPERLY

VISITED ALL THREE AIR LOCKS AND
FOUND THE CORRECT CODE, I WILL
CONFIRM THE CODE IS CORRECT ON
THAT PAGE AND THAT PAGE *ALONE.*
IF YOU DON'T SEE A NOTE FROM ME,
TURN BACK TO PAGE 1, AS OWEN
WILL HAVE ENTERED THE WRONG
CODE AND RESTARTED TIME FOR THE
ENTIRE PRISON.)

STAY IN BED. REST UP. YOU'RE GOING TO NEED IT.

The calming thought floated through his mind, and suddenly all the fear of the moment seemed to fade away. Things couldn't really be that bad. Why not just sleep for a few more hours and see how the world looked then?

Sure, that seemed like an odd thing to do, all things considered, but the drowsy feeling came on so powerfully, it was hard to fight.

"Maybe just five minutes," Owen whispered, and slowly felt himself slipping away into sleep.

Just as he drifted off, a loud voice split through his head, and his eyes flew open to find the entire room lit up.

"Good morning, prisoners. Welcome to the last day of your life!" said a voice from speakers in the ceiling, and Owen's eyes widened. He slowly pushed himself out of bed, the drowsiness now completely gone, and quietly slid over to what appeared to be an open jail cell door. He put his back to the wall, wondering a few things all at once:

Had Nobody stuck him in jail?

Why was the door open?

Who was this voice?

What did they mean, the last day of his life?

Turn to page 177. ◆〉

Owen stood in the small room by himself, ready to punch the wall, his older self, or anything else he could get his hands on. Why wouldn't this *work* for him? Future Owen had explained exactly how to do it, but no matter how hard he tried, Owen just couldn't open a page to another book.

"Just keep practicing—you'll get it," his future self told him before leaving with Kara to go over whatever it was that she had been panicking about earlier. Owen had considered pushing the issue and making them talk about it in front of him, but neither seemed to want him to know about the future, which was incredibly ironic, considering where they were.

"Imagine the book you want to travel to," Owen whispered to himself, repeating his future self's words. He brought to mind Jupiter City, with the Apathetic Industries building, the

Second Cousins headquarters, and the rest, picturing it in his head as clearly as he could. That part was all well and good. But the second part was the impossible bit.

"The fictional world was literally built by magic," his older self had said. "And you can use that. Science follows logical rules, uses implicit controls already existing within reality. But magic is chaos, and is open to anything if you ask the right way. That's how Nobody can rewrite himself. He views himself as a character in a story, and magic responds accordingly. If you believe that you're in a story now too, and need to pass between pages, the magic will make it happen. Just believe, and then ask."

I believe I'm going to beat up my older self the next time I see him. Why did this have to be so difficult? And hadn't it taken his future self ten years to figure it out, but now Owen was expected to somehow learn it in ten minutes? This wasn't going to work!

Sigh. He had to stop all of the negative thoughts. They weren't helping, even if no one but he and the readers would know about them. Weirdly, those readers might have come in handy right about now, if they chose to decide that he suddenly had the power to travel between stories. Of course, his older self had said he could invite them back, like a vampire or something, but that meant he'd lose control of his life again. So instead, they'd just stay up there reading, powerless to change the story.

Trust me, I know how it feels.

Okay, he had to try again. Owen closed his eyes and concentrated on Jupiter City, right down to the look of the cement in the sidewalks. Gritting his teeth, Owen raised a hand in the air, telling himself over and over that when he grabbed at nothing, this magic reality would rip like a page in a book and open a doorway into Doc Twilight's world. It would work. It *had* to work.

Owen closed his fingers on nothing, then slowly pulled down, hearing a ripping noise in his mind. Finally, he opened one eye, then growled in frustration.

No page, no doorway, *nothing*.

"I can't do this!" he shouted, flopping onto the cot face-first. He moaned into the mattress, then turned over, rubbing his palms into his eyes while mumbling evil things about magic. This was so *useless*.

And then something occurred to him. Why did he even have to learn, anyway? Couldn't his older self just open a page to

Jupiter City? It might be *easier* if Owen himself could do it, but it wasn't necessary.

Owen jumped up off the cot and threw open the door, wondering where Kara and older Owen had gone. Voices from across the hallway didn't sound like theirs, so Owen moved farther down, stopping to listen at each door. Most rooms were either empty or just silent (hard to tell which), but at the very last door he recognized Kara, and she didn't sound happy.

"It could happen at any time, then! Where am I right now?"

"The Countess has you," Owen's older self said. "She has more than one of your selves locked away in her prime time line, wherever that is. I've been searching for it for years, but I was never as good at this as you are, and I keep getting beaten by paradoxes. But I have one final plan that I think—"

"*No!*" Kara shouted at him. "Don't you get it, Owen? Whatever that plan is . . . you *know* what will happen. It's what always happens! No matter how I change the time lines, I can't fix this. I've tried so many things to stop it . . . all of my selves have. But nothing *works*."

"Kara, listen to me," his older self said. "You and I have had this conversation at least a thousand times. But I've done what I had to do with my younger self, and if I can help free this reality from the Countess, then it'll be worth it."

"I'm not letting you go. If the me of this time line isn't here to stop you, then *I* will."

There was a pause. "You can't stop me, Kara. And besides, if you stop the Countess from doing away with the TSA, none of this will even exist." He sighed. "I just wish I could give you the exact time the agency was founded, but I haven't been able to find it in all the years. How *she* ever found it is beyond me."

"All the more reason for me to stay and help you first. We'll free my older selves and then they can protect you while I take my Owen back and restart the TSA. It's the safest thing to do."

"No, it's not. Because the last thing I'm doing is putting you in danger. You're the only weapon we have against the Countess, and if you get taken too, that's it, that's the entire world, gone."

Okay, whatever all of this was, it was time for Owen to confront them and get the real truth. There were just too many hints about terrible things coming in the future, and honestly, Owen was really tired of it. He put his hand on the doorknob but froze before turning it when someone at the other end of the hall shouted.

At first he assumed the shout came from one of the other rooms, but those doors opened and a variety of people looked out in confusion, including a woman with an eye patch and a man covered in digital clock tattoos.

Owen stepped away from the door and moved down the hall with the crowd, trying to figure out where all the shouting was coming from. Not only loud voices, but metallic bangs, too, almost like . . . pots and pans?

The restaurant upstairs. Someone was there, and they weren't happy.

"Everyone, get out of here," the eye-patch woman shouted. "We've been discovered!"

The various rebels against the Countess all reached for their wrists, then pushed a button on their time bracelets. But nothing happened.

And then a robed, bald woman stepped down the stairs, with a host of robed people behind her, each one wearing a glowing glove.

"Destroy the dissidents!" shouted Dolores, the Countess's daughter, before turning to Owen. "But don't touch that boy.

He's with the devil girl, and I want to deliver them to my mother myself!"

"She blocked our time bracelets somehow!" the woman with the eye patch shouted. "We can't leave!"

Dolores smiled at that. And then she began to vibrate.

Turn to page 190. ⬧❯

Owen opened his eyes, his head pounding, and found himself in a small jail cell. His heart began racing, and for a moment he was terrified that the day had been reset again, all the way back to the time prison.

But this cell had no window. And the door was *definitely* not open.

A light came on, shining straight into his eyes. He winced, covering his face with his hand, then tried to see beyond the glare. "Hello?" he said.

"Where's the machine?" said a low, gruff male voice.

The machine? Did this person mean Kara's time bracelet? "I don't know," Owen said. "Where's my friend?"

"Where did you take the machine?" the voice said.

"What machine?" Owen asked. "Who are you?"

"You *know* who I am," the voice said, and a face pushed into the light: a boy with dark hair wearing a purple mask. "And you know what machine. You stole it from me, and I want it *back*."

Owen gasped. Was that Kid Twilight's costume? It looked exactly like the version he'd seen in Bethany's grandfather's house. This couldn't actually be Doc Twilight's sidekick, could it? The banana had mentioned something about him, now that he thought about it. "Um, I didn't steal anything. I just got here. I'm looking for my friends—"

"You're actually going to stick with the same story, after stealing from us?" the boy said, and something lashed out, hitting the bars hard enough to make them ring. Owen jumped back in surprise.

"I swear, I've never been here before, or ever met you," Owen told him. "How could I tell you the same story twice?"

The boy glared through his purple mask. "That's the most pathetic lie I've ever heard. I saw you with *my own eyes*. You claimed to be looking for your friends, and I believed you." He leaned forward again, gritting his teeth. "I took you at your word, and you stole the machine right out from under us!"

What was going on? Was this a time travel thing? Did he and Kara travel into the past and steal whatever machine it was that Kid Twilight was talking about? "Where is the girl who was with me?" Owen asked. "She'll back me up on all of this."

Kid Twilight moved his face from the light, and for a moment there was just silence. "She disappeared," he said finally. "I expect you figured Doc and I would be out tracking you down, so you thought it'd be safe to return. But that's why I stayed behind." He moved back into the light and looked almost as angry as if one of the Dark's shadows had taken him over. "And now Doc isn't answering my radio. I swear, if I got him back just for you to take him away again, I'll—"

"I'm telling you the truth!" Owen shouted, unsure how else to get through to this kid. "The Rotten Banana told us that this was the last place he saw my friends. I came here hoping to find some trace of them. One had a jet pack, another was half-robotic—"

Something hit the bars again hard. "Stop telling me the same story!" Kid Twilight shouted. "That's exactly what you said last time. I wrongly thought that if you knew Bethany and the others—"

"Wait, you met Bethany? Where is she?"

Kid Twilight glared at him. "Where do you think? You stole the machine we were using to bring her back!"

"Pretend I have no idea what you're talking about," Owen

said. "What happened when Bethany faced the Dark? The last I saw, he had her defeated, and—"

"The last you saw?" Kid Twilight said. "You were here for the fight?" He crossed his arms. "And yet you claimed you've never seen me before."

"No, I . . . it doesn't matter." Owen dropped his head into his hands. How could he explain the comic pages between worlds? Kid Twilight didn't believe a word he said anyway. It had to be time travel. But where was Kara?

"I'm going to ask you one more time," Kid Twilight said, and he stood up, moving into the light. In his hand he held a staff as long as he was, probably what he'd been hitting the bars with. "And if you don't tell me what I want to know . . ." He tapped the staff against the cell in a threatening manner. "Where. Is. The. Machine?"

"I don't know!" Owen shouted. "I have no idea. I don't even know what machine you're talking about!"

Kid Twilight nodded, then unlocked the cell door and pulled it open. He raised his staff to a striking position . . .

Then flew backward into the dark. Owen heard some scuffling, and something hit the floor hard. The staff banged against the ground, then again. After that was only silence.

Owen moved carefully to the door of his cell, ready to slam it closed in order to keep Kid Twilight away from him if it came to that. "Hello?" he said nervously.

"Sorry about that," Kara said, stepping into the light. "Had to catch my breath. That guy was *good*. Even with the time bracelet, he managed to anticipate me appearing twice!" She reached to the side of the cage and hit something, and lights turned on, revealing a large cavernlike room filled with computers and various superhero trophies.

Just a few feet from his cell, Kid Twilight lay on the ground unconscious. "That was *amazing*," Owen said, shaking his head. "How did you hide from him?"

"Something attacked us coming down the stairs," she said, grabbing Kid Twilight's cape and dragging him into the cell. "I had just enough time to hit the bracelet. I ended up a few thousand years in the future, so it took me a few seconds to get back." She half smiled at him. "You should see what this city looks like then, by the way. Everything's so futuristic. Duck museum's the same, though." She closed the cell door and fell back against the bars with a *whoof*. "When I got back, I didn't know how to unlock the cell, so I waited until he did before I made my move."

"Did you hear what he was saying?" Owen asked. "He claimed I stole something from him. Do you think maybe we come here again in the past?"

"It's possible," she said. "Maybe there's some footage or something? Places like this must have security cameras."

That made sense. Owen moved over to the giant computer on one wall, then tentatively pushed one of the buttons. The entire system turned on, and the largest monitor Owen had ever seen lit up.

"Awaiting voice command," the computer said. "That is, unless you don't actually need me and just woke me up to be cruel."

Huh. The computer's voice was sarcastic.

"I'd like to see what happened the last time I was here," Owen said.

Several light beams scanned over him. "Acknowledged," the computer said. "I didn't need a 'please,' either. You're welcome, of course."

"Um, thank you?" Owen said.

"Too late," the computer replied, and a video appeared on the screen.

A video of Owen talking to Kid Twilight.

Owen gasped. Kid Twilight hadn't been lying. There he was, shaking the sidekick's hand and speaking to a costumed man who must have been Doc Twilight. Had Bethany actually defeated the Dark in the end and restored her father?

There wasn't any sound, but the three quickly walked over to a small metal box near the computer monitor. The Owen on-screen touched it briefly, and light flared, too bright for Owen to see through. When everything returned to normal, both Doc and Kid Twilight were on the floor, and Owen was walking out with the box.

"Anything else, Your Majesty?" the computer asked. "Take your time; I have nothing better to be doing with my processor."

Before Owen could respond, the version of him on-screen looked up at the camera shooting the video. That Owen grinned widely and waved, then continued on his way. And suddenly Owen knew what had happened.

"Fowen?" he whispered.

Turn to page 304. ◆>

As Dolores's hand touched his chest, Owen desperately hoped the readers had fulfilled his request. Uncertain what else to do, he willed his entire body to just . . . *stop*, to completely freeze the entire thing in time. If Dolores could use his powers this way, then he could too, assuming the readers had agreed to it! And now even if Dolores stopped time around his heart, the rest of him would be frozen too, and no damage would be done. Then he'd be able to unfreeze all of himself later, and everything would be fine!

He closed his eyes, hoping he was right. That was the theory, at least. What if being frozen, though, he wasn't able to *un*freeze—

Instantly, Owen's entire body completely stopped.

And then, just as fast, it restarted again.

Oh no! Had it not worked? Owen opened his eyes, expecting to see Dolores about to time-freeze his heart. Instead, though,

Kara was kneeling at his side looking both worried and hopeful, while a man in a uniform sat next to her, holding Owen's wrist to take his pulse.

"Um, did I miss something?" Owen asked, looking around the room. Both the Countess and her daughter were gone, while the robot TIME-R seemed to be fine. "Or a whole lot of somethings?"

Kara just stared at him for a moment, then, with a joyful whoop, tackled him with a hug hard enough to smack him back to the ground. "You're *alive!*" she shouted again and again.

"You were frozen in time, kid," the uniformed man told him, releasing Owen's wrist. "How exactly did that happen?"

Owen coughed, then lowered himself back to the ground, pretending to still be weak from the freezing process. He didn't really want to get into his powers with whoever this guy was. "One . . . one minute. Can you . . . tell me what happened here first?"

TIME-R reached out and pushed a button on one of the laboratory computers, and security footage began playing on all the screens. The scene started with Dolores touching Owen, and his entire body going completely still.

"Funny, they're not usually so quiet," said the Dolores on the screens as she stood up and gave Owen's body an odd look. She kicked him with her foot, then frowned. "You'd think he'd be in pain—"

"You monster!" Kara screamed at Dolores, moving to Owen's side and placing her hand on his heart. She paused, then shouted in rage. Tears falling, Kara balled her hands together, then brought them down on Owen's chest over and over, yelling for him to wake up. Back in the present, Owen winced, putting a hand over his heart. Hopefully, since it was frozen, Kara hadn't been able to hurt it.

"Dolores, what did I tell you?" the Countess on the monitors said, her gloved hand hovering over TIME-R. "I can barely hear myself think! Could you *do* something about her?"

Kara hit Owen's chest one more time, then collapsed to his side, sobbing loudly. Dolores bent down to grab her, but Kara just turned to look at her with absolute hatred in her eyes, and the bald woman took a surprised step back.

"You have no idea what you've done," Kara said. She wiped her eyes with her hand, then pushed herself to her feet. "You've just unleashed the end of the entire world, and for the very first time, *I'm going to welcome it.*"

"What are you talking about?" the Countess said, moving away from TIME-R. "Don't be foolish, Kara. You're powerless here."

"I *am* powerless," she said, taking a step toward Dolores, who backed away from her slowly. "I've been trying to fight this prophecy for a year now, and I've failed each time. But now I'm going to embrace it. The world can burn for all I care. I'd rather that than let you rule it, even for a minute!"

"Kill her, Dolores," the Countess said, and her daughter raised a tentative hand toward Kara's heart.

Kara leaped forward, grabbed Dolores's hand, and yanked it to her chest. "Do it! It won't stop the end of all time. Whatever you do to me, my future selves will still end this reality. This I promise you."

The Countess sighed. "Her and her immunity to paradox," the Countess said. "She's bluffing, anyway."

"What if she's not?" Dolores asked, trying to pull her hand away. Kara held it fast, though, and took another step closer to her.

"Go look and see, if you're so gullible!" the Countess roared. "Travel into the future and see what she's done!"

Dolores nodded and yanked her hand away, then disappeared, only to reappear an instant later, clearly terrified. "She's not bluffing. There's nothing there, Mother! It's all just a white nothingness. She's going to destroy it all!"

"Impossible!" the Countess shouted. "Kill her now and be done with this!"

But Dolores shook her head. "What if it doesn't stop her? We can't take that chance. We need to keep her locked up!" She turned to the robot strapped to the table. "We must allow the TSA to form if there's any hope at all."

The Countess turned white in shock. "That might be the most dull-witted suggestion you've ever dared make," she said, bringing her glove back to TIME-R. "I cannot believe any offspring of mine could be so pathetic!"

Dolores's eyes widened. "Mother, I—"

"No! I won't hear one more sound from that hideous bald head of yours. You've wasted too much of my precious time here already, and I won't have it anymore. I won't!"

"Mother, *you need to listen*—"

"To you? Every sentence you utter drops my intelligence by ten percent."

Dolores balled her hands into fists. "Mother, stop—"

"You will not order ME around, you miserable little fool!" the Countess shouted. "I rue the day that you were ever born, and—"

Dolores shrieked incoherently, then leaped forward and slapped her mother.

The Countess had just enough time to manage a truly shocked expression before she toppled over like a tree falling in the woods, her body frozen in time. "Just *shut up* for once, you evil old hag!" her daughter yelled over her still body. "I'm right about this, and you're wrong. Did you hear me, Mother? YOU'RE WRONG!" She kicked her mother's frozen leg. "Wrong, wrong, wrong, wrong, wrong, you horrible, despicable monster!"

Taking a deep breath, Dolores moved to the table and unstrapped TIME-R. "There," she said to the robot, waving it forward. "Go and do what you were meant to. You're welcome."

TIME-R rose up off the table, studied her for a moment, then grabbed her with his metal arms, holding her tightly in place. "YOU THREATEN THE PEACE OF THIS ERA WITH YOUR ACTIONS," TIME-R declared. "CLEARLY, THERE IS A NEED FOR A FORCE FOR JUSTICE THROUGH-OUT THE TIMESTREAM, GIVEN WHAT I HAVE WITNESSED HERE TODAY. I SHALL HENCEFORTH ESTABLISH AN AGENCY TO POLICE SUCH CRIMES—"

"What?" Dolores said. "Are you saying that *we* caused the TSA to be created?" She groaned in annoyance. "This is all Mother's fault!"

TIME-R tapped her on the head, and Dolores instantly

fell unconscious. The robot gently laid her on the floor as two women and one man in gray suits blinked into existence on either side of him. One woman grabbed the Countess, the other took Dolores, and both disappeared as the man in the suit stepped over to Owen.

"Looks like we've got a five thirty-eight here," the man said, running a piece of glass over Owen's body. "Frozen in time. Shouldn't take much to restart him."

"What did you say?" Kara said softly, then moved to the other side of Owen. "He's . . . he's not dead?"

"Nope, he'll be fine," the man said. He placed a time bracelet on Owen's wrist, then fiddled with the buttons. "Just have to kick him back into the proper timestream." He looked up at her, then gasped. "Kara *Dox*?!" He grabbed his collar and started speaking into it. "Time Security agent on the scene, responding to the seven seven seven, the founder found. Third suspect is Kara Dox, and—"

"I'll go quietly, okay?" she said, holding her hands out in surrender. "Just . . . just fix him! Do whatever it takes. If I can help at all, I will. Just make him be okay!"

The agent stared at her for another moment, then tapped the time bracelet on Owen's wrist.

Immediately Owen sat up and looked all around him. "Um, did I miss something?" he whispered to Kara. "Or a whole lot of somethings?"

TIME-R shut off the monitors, having reached the present, and Owen let out a deep breath, feeling an incredible weight lift off of his body. They'd actually done it! They'd defeated the Countess and her daughter, restarted the TSA, and he hadn't even had to actually die in the process! Was this what winning felt like? It'd been so long since he'd experienced anything like it. For a moment, he just let it sink in, smiling peacefully.

"How did you know this would work?" Kara asked him quietly, and the peaceful feeling immediately disappeared.

"I, um, didn't," Owen said, looking embarrassed. "I was hoping that Dolores was as gullible as you say I am, so I just froze myself. Figured that'd keep her from murdering me. After that, I thought you could bluff your way out with the whole world ending . . ." He trailed off, wincing as the TSA agent leaned in with interest.

The agent rolled his eyes. "I just watched the same tape you did, son. I heard everything. I'm going to have to take you in, Ms. Dox. You're supposed to be in the Jules Verne Memorial Time Prison right now. Escape from the prison adds a year to your sentence." He frowned. "Weird rule, I know, since you're already there forever. So now I suppose you're there for infinity plus one year."

What? After everything they'd done, the TSA still wanted to throw Kara in jail? Owen tensed his body, ready to attack or grab a time bracelet or something, but the robot interrupted his plans.

"THESE TWO PROTECTED ME," TIME-R said, helping Owen to his feet. "GIVEN THAT IT CLEARLY APPEARS I AM SUCCESSFUL IN MY EFFORTS TO BUILD A TIME SECURITY AGENCY, I GRANT THEM BOTH CLEMENCY AT THIS TIME AS A REWARD."

"But, sir," the agent started. "You don't know who this *is*. This is Kara Dox. Immune to paradox after her mother gave birth to her in a time bubble. Her older self has caused no less than three hundred and twelve reported time violations, including fourteen major time felonies. We have reason to believe she's at the heart of reality disappearing a century from now. The future itself is being destroyed, sir, and—"

Kara reached over and took Owen's hand in hers. "Hold on," she whispered, then touched the buttons on the time bracelet still on his wrist. Before the agent or TIME-R could react, Owen and Kara disappeared from the room, reappearing back by the same café where they'd arrived before facing the Countess. Now, though, the café looked a bit newer, and people were driving the cars instead of using their phones (well, most of them).

Just like that, they'd escaped. Another wave of relief washed over him, and he fell into one of the café's chairs with a sigh. Crises were averted, and the good guys emerged victorious for once! Now all he needed to do . . .

All he needed to do was rescue a missing half-fictional girl from an all-powerful Nobody who could literally do or be anything. The weight of this crashed down on him, and he slumped in the chair, feeling even more anxious than before, now that Kara's immediate problems had passed.

"We're back in your present," Kara told him, fiddling with the time bracelet. "I'm blocking their tracking, so we should be okay for a few minutes at least." She looked away. "So I . . . I guess that's it, then. Last time this was easier, because I could just leave a note, but—"

"What are you talking about?" he asked her.

"You need to go take care of your business with Nobody," she said. "And I . . . I need to get back into the time prison."

What? She was going to turn *herself* back in again? "But why?" Owen asked. "Your prophecy just came true, and I'm still here!"

"But the future isn't," Kara said. "And we both know that's my fault somehow. I told you, no matter how I try to fix things, the universe finds a way." She stepped forward and hugged him tightly. "There's no other choice. Now you need to go and find your friend, okay?" She released him, gave him one last look, then began to play with the buttons on the time bracelet.

No! She *couldn't* just do this to herself, not again! He needed an argument, something she'd believe, but there was no time to think, and he couldn't—

OWEN SHOULD SAY THAT TRAVELING WITH HIM TO ANOTHER STORY WILL NEGATE HER DESTINY.

Turn to page 8.

OWEN SHOULD SAY THAT HE'LL NEVER SEE HER AGAIN IF SHE GOES, AND HE CAN'T TAKE THAT.

Turn to page 91.

OWEN SHOULD SAY THAT THEY'LL FIND A WAY TO FIX THINGS IN THE FUTURE, THEY JUST NEED SOME TIME.

Turn to page 180.

K yoto in the year 10,000," Kara said, grabbing Owen's
hand and hitting the bracelet.

They jumped forward in time, only to appear in the middle
of nothing. Everything was blank, a white world absent of anything, just like the space between stories.

"Wait, what happened?" Kara said. "The time bracelet says
we're in the correct year, but this can't be the same place."

What did this mean? The world was just . . . gone. Had
Nobody split the fictional and nonfictional worlds, and this
was the result?

"Something's *very* wrong," Kara said.

"It sure is," said a voice, and they whirled around to find
Dolores with several robed guards. She immediately touched
Owen and Kara on the neck, and they both collapsed to the
ground.

The last thing Owen heard was Dolores's voice getting farther and farther away. "Bring them, but keep them asleep. The Countess doesn't want them to wake up before she disposes of them."

Readers, turn back now! This is the . . . the wrong . . .

And then everything went dark.

Owen screamed as the T. rex launched at him, then squeezed his eyes shut and put up his arms in defense, waiting for the worst.

But nothing happened.

Owen lowered his arms, his eyes still closed. How could nothing have happened? He had to be dead, eaten, gone. But in spite of a terrible smell coming from somewhere, he seemed to be no different than a second before.

Owen slowly opened one eye, ready for anything. Except, that was, for what he saw: the inside of the T. rex's mouth.

"AHH! AHH! AHH!" he shouted over and over like the alarm in the air lock. He began hyperventilating and couldn't move or think. He was inside the dinosaur's mouth. *He was inside the dinosaur's mouth!*

"Sounds like you're still alive," the bald woman shouted from somewhere near his feet.

Owen screamed once more, then sort of trailed off, feeling very dizzy after all the screaming. He reached out a hand to steady himself, then yanked it back when he felt the dinosaur's wet cheek against his fingers. Another wave of panic hit him, but this time he took deep breaths and held it back.

"We don't have much time here," the woman reminded him, poking her head up inside the T. rex's mouth from below, "and I can't fit in there. You're going to need to get the code."

"What?" Owen shouted at her, wanting to kick her, if only he had enough room between the teeth to do so. "I can't even move!"

She shifted around, trying to get a better look. "Sure you can. It's not even touching you. There are at least six inches between the teeth and your legs. Just crawl up."

"Crawl? On its tongue?!"

"I told you to make sure you left me room," the woman told him. "So this is *your* fault. Better hurry now, you've only got about thirty seconds to get the code and get out before time starts again. Not to mention you'll probably want to get out of its range after that—"

"Okay!" Owen shouted as he put a hand on the T. rex's wavy tongue, cringing at the slimy texture. He pulled his hand away to wipe it on his shirt, then realized it wasn't exactly going to get any better. So instead, he jumped up and grabbed the tongue with both arms, hugging it close to him to pull himself up. "GAH," he shouted, inching his way farther toward the back of the creature's throat, his face wiping along the tongue.

"It shouldn't be too far back there," Owen heard the woman shout from below. "Twenty seconds left."

Owen inched forward, trying his best to see in the low light while ignoring the smell. Why couldn't the smell be frozen in time too? If he ever met the prison builders, that was the first thing he'd complain about. Well, right after forcing prisoners to get eaten by dinosaurs.

The tongue leveled out as the T. rex's head narrowed, leaving Owen to squirm forward like he was in a tunnel just barely larger than his body. Not seeing the code, Owen picked his head up to look around, only to bang it against a large fleshy thing hanging down in the creature's throat.

"Ow!" he shouted, then carefully moved his head so he could see. The uvula glistened in the remaining light, and right in the middle of it was a large numeral "0."

"I've got it!" Owen shouted, pushing himself back down as quickly as he could.

"Yell it out to me!" the bald woman said. "You're not going to make it, only ten seconds!"

"NO!" Owen shouted as he landed back on his feet. *Nine. Eight.* He tried sliding through the dinosaur's sharp teeth without cutting himself, but there was no time. *Seven. Six.* Instead, he just pushed himself out as fast as possible, leaving ugly cuts on his arms and legs.

Five. Four. Three. He hit the ground and rolled out from under the T. rex. The bald woman had reached the air lock already and was watching from a safe distance.

Two. One. Owen pushed to his feet and sprinted as fast as he could as time kicked in.

The Tyrannosaurus's jaws closed shut with a crash. It turned, saw its prey fleeing, and roared loudly. Owen didn't look back, but could feel the ground shaking as it pounded after him.

"Tell me the code!" the bald woman shouted from the air lock's safety. "It's going to catch you. You have no chance!"

Owen just shook his head, running with all of his might, his entire body shaking with fear. Whether or not the dinosaur ate him, he just hoped that it somehow managed to choke down the Countess's daughter, too.

The monster's steps got closer and closer, and Owen knew the woman was right, there was no way he could make it, he was doomed, it had to be on top of him . . .

And then he exploded into the air lock, almost plowing through two prisoners standing right in his way.

Owen collapsed to the floor, just trying to catch his breath. Was that it? Was he safe? He was so tired, he couldn't even look, and instead pushed himself to one of the walls and leaned back against it. He looked up, wondering why no one else had said anything, and finally realized that none of the prisoners had moved since he entered. In fact, they seemed to be frozen as well.

Ah, he'd kicked in his time powers! He smacked his forehead, realizing he could have been using them all along . . . like when the T. rex was trying to bite him, in fact!

"Agh," he said, dropping his head into his hands. He'd almost died, and never even *thought* about the powers. But that at least explained how he made it into the air lock.

"So?" the bald woman said, stepping in front of him. "What's the code? Tell me or I make sure you don't get out of here alive."

Owen opened his mouth to say it, then realized something. "How are you not . . . frozen?"

The woman slowly smiled. "You think I don't know who you are, Owen Conners? I know all about you, and your power to speed up your own time. Took me years to duplicate it . . . but while experimenting, I figured out how to slow people down, too." She put a finger near his neck. "I'm going to guess you haven't gotten that far yet. Now, the code?"

For a moment, Owen considered lying to her. But somehow, she'd know. He *knew* she'd know. "It was a zero," he said.

She stared at him for a moment, then nodded. "Right. Now, if you'll excuse me, I have to try to find a way out of here and get to the other challenges. Don't worry, you won't remember anything about me tomorrow." She touched her fingers to his neck, and Owen collapsed to the ground.

As blackness overtook him, one thought went through his mind. *Readers. The second digit. It's a zero. Don't forget. Second digit . . . is a zero.*

And then everything went dark.

TURN BACK TO PAGE 1 . . . OR

CHEAT A BIT, AND SKIP AHEAD TO

THE DECISIONS ON PAGE 259.

Owen glanced down at himself and made another odd discovery. Now that the lights were on, he noticed that instead of his normal clothes, he was now wearing an orange jumpsuit, just like a prisoner would wear. Next to his bed were a pair of shoes that looked about the right size, as well as gray socks and what Owen really hoped was a pair of clean underwear.

"Due to your actions breaking the time code, you are now a permanent inhabitant of the Jules Verne Memorial Time Prison," the soft, warm voice continued from the speakers overhead.

The *what*, now? Owen looked back down at his orange jumpsuit and noticed something else: It had SMITH printed on the upper right. If that was someone's name, it didn't bode well for any of these clothes being his. But where were his clothes?

And worse, who had dressed him? He shuddered.

"The Jules Verne Memorial Time Prison is located within the Cretaceous period of Earth's prehistory," the voice said as Owen put on the socks and shoes. "You have probably noticed the local flora and fauna outside of your cell window. Please, for the sake of the animals as well as your own health, keep all hands, feet, and legs inside your cell at all times. The animals have a specific diet, and we have no wish to change history by giving them a taste of human beings."

Animals? In the prehistoric era? Owen's eyes widened, and for the first time things seemed slightly less awful. Those were *dinosaurs* outside! And the roaring had been close. Could he actually see real-life dinosaurs if he looked? Or at least the fictional versions that whoever had written this story had come up with?

Something nagged at his memory about all of this, but it couldn't be that important. Mostly, in spite of the voice's warning, how often did you get to see real live dinosaurs? What could it hurt just to look, after all?

**MAKE OWEN LOOK OUT THE WINDOW
FOR DINOSAURS.**

Turn to page 87. ◆❯

**QUIT WASTING TIME. OWEN SHOULD
TRY TO FIND OUT HOW HE GOT HERE.**

Turn to page 278. ◆❯

*T*ELL KARA THAT YOU'LL HAVE PLENTY OF TIME TO FIX THINGS IN THE FUTURE. IT WON'T START DISAPPEARING FOR, LIKE, A CENTURY, THE AGENT SAID!

The thought hit Owen so hard he opened his mouth to say it before he even realized it. "We'll have plenty of time before . . . ," he said, then trailed off. *Hey!* he thought at the readers. *Can we maybe not focus on the world ending here when she blames herself for it?*

Still, the first part of the idea itself wasn't that bad. Owen moved to face Kara and grabbed her by her shoulders. "There's plenty of time to figure out another way out of all this," he said. "You don't need to go back to that prison!"

She shook her head. "You always say that, but it doesn't work, Owen. All of my future selves have tried, and they've all failed. Time won't solve anything." She sighed. "In fact, time's the only problem here."

Well, that didn't work. *I need something else to try! Any other suggestions?*

OWEN SHOULD SAY THAT LEAVING WITH HIM TO ANOTHER STORY WOULD FIX THINGS.

Turn to page 8. ⬍❯

OWEN SHOULD SAY THAT HE'LL NEVER SEE HER AGAIN IF SHE GOES, AND HE CAN'T LIVE WITHOUT HER.

Turn to page 91. ⬍❯

DINOSAUR! YOU HAVE TO PET IT!

Alarm bells rang through Owen's head as he slipped his hand between the bars of the window, but they weren't loud enough to stop him.

A low growl rumbled out of the jungle, and it echoed in Owen's chest, pulling him out of his trance. *What was he doing*, sticking his hand out the window? Why had he thought this was a good idea?!

The creature in the jungle lunged forward and Owen screamed, shoving himself backward as overpoweringly horrific breath hit him full blast. He tumbled off the bed and hit the floor hard. The massive creature slammed its head into the wall hard enough to crumble the rock wall around the bars.

Owen screamed again, scrambling backward from the window as the monster rammed its head into the bars over and over before finally giving up and moving one enormous eye to stare at Owen through the bars, a few of which were barely intact.

And then the creature disappeared, its heavy steps shaking the floor even inside his room.

Why had he done that? Was some part of him insane? He'd almost gotten his arm bitten off, if not more than that! What had he been thinking?

DON'T LET OWEN THINK ABOUT IT TOO HARD. LET'S GET BACK TO FIGURING OUT WHY HE'S HERE.

Turn to page 278. ⬍〉

allahassee in the year 2000," Kara said, grabbing Owen's hand and hitting the bracelet.

They instantly jumped backward in time, and landed in what looked to be a very similar time to the present.

That made sense. The year 2000 wasn't too long ago, after all. Weirdly, though, there were a few surprising differences that Owen would never have thought about. Cell phones were enormous, for one. And everyone's clothing was a lot brighter than he was used to. Other than that, though, nothing looked too out of place.

"This doesn't feel right," Kara said.

"I wouldn't imagine so," said a voice, and they whirled around to find Dolores with several robed guards. She immediately touched Owen and Kara on the neck, and they both collapsed to the ground.

The last thing Owen heard was Dolores's voice getting farther and farther away. "Bring them, but keep them asleep. The Countess doesn't want them to wake up before she disposes of them."

Readers, turn back now! This is the . . . the wrong . . .

And then everything went dark.

*T*HIS IS INSANE. WAIT UNTIL THE T. REX LEAVES!

See? Even the readers agreed!

Except apparently Kara hadn't gotten the blaring, headache-inducing thought, as she started toward the robot. Owen grabbed her arm and held her back. "Are you kidding?" he said. "We can't go over there!"

"I think I get what he's saying," Kara told him. "If the T. rex is just now . . . RUN!"

"Just now AAH!" Owen shouted as she yanked him to the ground. Two six-foot-tall dinosaurs passed backward right over the spot he'd just been in, looking like they were running from the T. rex.

"Whoa!" Owen said, and looked up just in time to get slammed in the head by a third creature's tail. His eyes rolled back into his head, and he fell back to the dirt floor, unconscious.

Readers, you just changed the entire backward time line. If Owen had been living this forward, he would have made it all the way from the air lock to the volcano, so he couldn't have been knocked out at this point. Basically, you have just created a paradox that might have ended time entirely, if not for Kara's presence. Please be a bit more careful next time. Turn back to page 1. (Or cheat a bit and turn back to page 35.)

*H*ELP HER!

The thought pounded in his head, but Owen barely heard it, as he was already moving. He slammed into the bald woman from behind, knocking her to the ground, then jumped up onto the table next to Kara, ready to kick anyone who got close.

"What are you doing?" Kara shouted, her eyes on the advancing crowd of prisoners instead of on Owen. "You were supposed to escape!"

"I couldn't just leave you like this," he told her. One of the prisoners grabbed for his foot, but he kicked the man's hand and began circling Kara on the table.

"I'll be fine tomorrow morning, no matter what," Kara told him. "Go now! It's not too late!"

But it was. A group of prisoners moved to block the door,

while hands shot out and grabbed both Owen and Kara, ripping their feet out from under them. Both hit the table hard, and Owen felt a little woozy as prisoners carried them to the Countess and held them before her.

She smiled down on them evilly. "Now, children," she said. "This might all be reversed at the stroke of twelve, but believe me, I'll enjoy taking your time. If you have any memory of it, tell me tomorrow what it's like to turn to dust."

And with that, she touched her glove to Owen's cheek.

I appreciate your noble impulses, readers, but this story doesn't seem to allow for them. It's almost as if Owen's presence here negates any good you might wish to do. Either way, turn back to page 1, or try your choice again on page 132.

As Dolores began to disappear from view, Owen instantly recognized his own time power. Not sure what else to do, he quickly kicked his power into gear, his body vibrating faster and faster as everything began to slow down around him. Everything except Dolores, who blurred back into sight as he matched her speed.

"It's been too many years, boy," the bald woman said, slipping between the now-frozen rebellious time travelers. As she passed each one, she reached out and flicked them in the forehead, which seemed ominous.

Owen tried to think of a brave, intimidating response. "It's only been a few *hours* for me," he said, glaring at her threateningly.

She smiled, touching the eye-patch woman's neck. "Do you know how many years I spent trying to re-create your powers?

Mother thought it was a fool's errand, of course. But I gathered the finest scientists I could find in all the future and put them to work. It still took them over a decade."

And it took Charm maybe twenty minutes while in the middle of fighting shadows and giving his friends superpowers, too. "Maybe they just weren't very smart."

"Since then, though, I've had quite a bit of time to practice with it," she said, and disappeared.

Owen's eyes widened and he looked all around him, but Dolores was nowhere to be seen. Where had she—

Something hit him, and he slammed against the wall to his right. Before he could react, another hit knocked him into the opposite wall, and he collapsed to the ground, trying to breathe.

"See?" Dolores said, reappearing right above him. She leaned over and grinned. "Not so fast anymore, are you?"

"Still fast enough . . . ," Owen said, struggling to his feet, "to outrun—"

She disappeared again, and what felt like ten, a hundred, maybe a thousand kicks pounded into Owen's stomach, so fast they felt like a constant hit. He doubled over in pain and collapsed to the ground again.

"I'm sorry, you were saying?" Dolores asked, crouching down on the floor next to him. "You know, I wouldn't normally strike a child. But you're *special*. You've had this coming ever since you betrayed my mother in the time prison." She grinned. "You skipped your punishment then, but justice always finds you in the end, Owen Conners."

Owen groaned, agony filling every corner of his mind. He needed to get help, but how? He couldn't even move fast enough to escape from the woman, let alone find anyone who could possibly stand up to her. If he could just reach Kara, maybe they could time jump . . . except whatever was interfering with the other time travelers' bracelets would nullify Kara's, too.

"No more tough talk?" Dolores asked, still lying next to him. "That won't do. Let me get you back on your feet." She stood up, then grabbed Owen by his armpits and yanked him to a standing position, only for him to weakly fall back against the wall for support.

Dolores disappeared for a second, then turned up again, time bracelets running up and down her arm. "Look what I found," she said, showing them off to Owen. "The last of the rebels' time machines. Now, what should I do to these, I wonder?"

Owen eyed the bracelets. He had to stop her. Without the

bracelets, Owen's older self and the others would not only be stuck here in this time, but they'd never be able to find the older Kara or the Countess. They'd be sitting ducks for Dolores and the Countess's guards. He couldn't let her just get away with this. The fact that she and her mother were free was because of him, after all. There had to be something he could do to fix this!

And maybe there was. If she could move faster . . . then so could he. Owen closed his eyes and willed himself to move even quicker.

Dolores leaned in closer. "This is adorable. You're trying to speed up, aren't you!" She grabbed his hand, and Owen gasped as energy pulsated through him, sending his heart racing. "Don't worry, boy. I'll help you out."

Owen began to see spots as his robotic heart beat faster and faster. "What are . . . you doing?" he asked, his vision narrowing until all he could see was Dolores's face.

"You wanted to go faster, so I'm adding my speed to yours," she whispered in his ear. "Now I'm going to be generous and give you a thousandth-of-a-second head start. If you can reach the door where Kara is before me, then I'll let you two go." She giggled softly. "But if I win, then she's all *mine*."

She let go of Owen and stood back as he practically exploded with vibrating energy, then she raised her hand like she was starting a race. "Ready?" she asked.

He nodded, the entire hallway pulsing in his sight.

"Go!" she shouted, and dropped her hand.

The distance to the end of the hall couldn't have been more than twenty feet, but the way he was feeling, Owen wasn't sure he'd last five. He exploded toward the door, sprinting as fast as he could, feeling like he'd had all the sugar and soda in the world. His heartbeat echoed in his vision and hearing as he ran, and the air in front of him kept popping for some reason.

None of it was enough.

When he was still ten feet away, something burst past him, and Dolores reappeared at the door, leaning against it casually like she'd been waiting for hours. Owen stumbled to a stop, then fell to his knees, hoping his robotic heart wouldn't break from all of this speed. His entire body screamed with soreness, like he'd just run a few marathons, even though he'd barely made it ten feet.

"Oh, c'mon," Dolores said, standing over him. "I'm trying to torture you here, and you can't even run a short distance. Where's the fun in that?"

"You're a monster," Owen told her. He forced himself to slow down as much as he could until all that was left was the time energy that Dolores had given him. His heart began to beat more slowly, and he took a deep breath in, trying not to think about what was going to happen. Not only had he just failed to save himself and Kara, but there was now no way he'd ever get back to Bethany or stop Nobody. He'd let down two entire worlds.

"Monster or not, you just lost the race," she told him, grinning widely. "Do you know what that means?"

"Don't touch her," Owen said, and attempted to push himself to his feet, but his muscles wouldn't respond.

"Who's going to stop me? You?" Dolores asked, still standing over him. "I dare you. I *dare* you. Stop me before I get to the door, Owen. You can't even move! Do it! Try to stop me! *Do—*"

And then Dolores went crashing down the hallway, plowing into the assembled robed guards.

Owen looked up to find his older self fading in and out of view, moving almost too fast to see. "You might have won the last time we raced, Dolores," he said. "But now it's time for a rematch."

Turn to page 328. ⬍⟩

*N*o!" Kara shouted into the jungle, her hands clenched into fists. "Where did it go? Where did the prison *go*, Owen?!"

He shook his head. How could it have just vanished like that? Was it invisible? Owen put his hands up and walked forward, but didn't run into anything. "I don't get it. What could have happened?"

Kara turned away from him, hands grabbing her head. "It must have been the Countess! I don't know how, but she must have stopped it from ever being built. But there's no way she could have done that. It was too big a deal! She would have had to infiltrate the entire Time Security Agency, if not—"

And then Kara went silent, standing motionless for a moment, her mouth hanging open. "No," she said finally, grabbed the bracelet off of Owen's hand, and disappeared.

Before Owen could even blink, Kara reappeared, looking just as upset as when she'd left.

"It's *gone*," Kara said, falling to the ground, not even looking at him. She dropped her head into her hands and shook it. "The entire agency . . . just gone. It never existed now. It was never even created."

"What?" Owen said. "But how can that be? The prison was here. Those two agents were here! Someone had to put *you* here. And you remember the agency, so how could it have never existed?"

"I'm immune to paradox," Kara whispered almost too softly for him to hear. "Time distortions don't affect me."

"But they affect *me*!" Owen shouted, his voice causing the nearby insects to go quiet. Remembering the large roaring creature outside his cell window back when the prison existed, he took a deep breath and lowered his voice. "This can't be real, Kara. You can't just make something not ever have existed!"

"The Countess must have found the agency's founder," Kara said, shaking her head. "But there's no way she could have. I mean, all agents' origins are kept hidden for just this reason, but the founder's identity is their greatest secret. The rumor is that the agency locked the founder away, just so no one could ever find him or her, even though a lot of people tried." She sighed. "I think my future self even looked."

"So the Countess, what, just killed this founder, and now there's no longer a TSA? No one is guarding time from time travelers?"

"I knew this would happen," Kara said, her voice barely loud enough for Owen to hear it. "The moment I'm out of the prison, it all falls apart."

He leaned down and grabbed her hand. "It's not safe here. Even if the Countess doesn't come after us, there are plenty of hungry dinosaurs out there." Not to mention that they had to return to the present and find a way back to Jupiter City.

Kara nodded, then stood up. She fiddled with the buttons on the bracelet, then turned to him, her eyes red around the edges. "I'm going to get you to safety first," she said, taking his hand. "After that . . . . I don't even know. I thought I could fix things by hiding in here. I thought I could take control of my life." She clenched her teeth, breathing slowly in and out. "But you can't fight destiny, can you? All of this power to travel through time, and I can't fix the one thing I need to. I can't stop the future."

"What . . . what is going to happen, Kara?" Owen asked.

She looked up at him again and forced a smile. "Trust me, Owen. You're the very last person who I'll ever tell. Now let's go. I want to get us as far from this place as possible, just in case anyone tries to find us." She touched the bracelet. "Moving slowly through time creates less of a disruption in the continuum, so it's harder to track. For that reason, we won't just jump to another time. We'll coast for a bit, then speed up as we get farther away. As to where, here's what I think we should do . . ."

Kara trailed off, like she was waiting for something. Was Owen supposed to say something, or . . . wait. *No.* This was another reader choice, wasn't it . . .

KARA SUGGESTS THEY GO AS FAR INTO THE FUTURE AS THEY CAN.

Turn to page 206. ⬩⟩

KARA SUGGESTS GOING BACK TO THE VERY BEGINNING OF TIME.

Turn to page 341. ⬩⟩

Congratulations, readers. This is indeed the correct code.

Give it to Owen and see what happens.

200. *THAT'S THE CODE. PUT IT IN BEFORE IT'S TOO LATE!*

Owen's foot stopped in midair as he moved to help Kara. The thought couldn't be ignored, but even so, he fought to keep going.

"Go!" Kara shouted at him as prisoners began to surround her table.

"Forget about her—that one's trying to put in a code!" the Countess shouted, pointing at Owen.

All of the prisoners surrounding Kara turned in Owen's direction, and he took a step back, not needing any readers to tell him what to do. There wasn't any choice anymore. The exit door was now his only chance.

Owen leaped to the code box and quickly plugged in 200, hoping that the readers were right. He mashed the Enter button hard, then frantically pushed on the door.

The door didn't open.

Glancing back over his shoulder, Owen saw the other prisoners just feet away, their arms reaching for him in eerie silence now. "C'mon!" he shouted, and threw himself against the door, his entire body shaking from the impact. Again and again, he crashed against the door, but it didn't move.

Finally, he gave up and turned around, his back to the wall, ready to fight.

Except the prisoners weren't any closer. In fact, they weren't moving at all and were just standing frozen in place. What had happened? Had he accidentally turned on his time powers?

Taking in a deep breath, Owen leaned against the wall, just glad to have a minute of relief. Unfortunately, he didn't get it, as the exit door next to him opened and two people stepped out into the prison.

A man and woman wearing gray one-piece suits looked around, each one wearing something that looked like a police badge, only with a clock in the center of it. They also seemed to have a sort of aura around them, a glowing light like the one that sometimes appeared around streetlights at night.

"How did this happen?" the man yelled at the woman. "You assured me that they'd never guess the correct code!"

"The whole prison is set up to keep them from doing so!" the woman said, rubbing her temples. "Ugh, look at all of them. I had no idea we were keeping so many of them in here now."

"They've been sending new ones for hundreds of years," the man said, stepping past Owen, who stayed as still as possible. If he was using his powers, then how were *they* speeding up their own time? What was going on?

"At least the exit door protocol still works," the man said, looking around at all the frozen prisoners. "One of them gets the door open, and time slows almost to a stop in the entire prison. That should give us enough time to straighten everything up and remove the problem."

Wait. Exit protocols? So this *wasn't* Owen speeding up his own time? But no, he would have to be, since the rest of the prison had slowed down. The agents' suits must have the same sort of effect as his powers, if they let them walk around normally as well.

"Since when did we start sending children?" the woman asked, gesturing at Owen. He kept still and held his breath as the agents approached him, trying not to think about how much he wanted to blink and scratch his nose at the same time. "What could he possibly have done?"

The man clicked something on his wrist that Owen couldn't

see, then frowned. "The only child we've sent here . . . was *Kara Dox*." His eyes widened as he said the name, and the woman next to him shuddered. "You know she had something to do with this. Why they thought she'd stay locked up is beyond me."

"If she's supposed to be here, where is she?" the woman asked.

They couldn't see Kara? Last Owen had looked, she was standing pretty obviously on top of a table. Had she moved? The worst thing was, he couldn't even turn his head to see, as they might notice he wasn't frozen.

"Find her," the man said, and started going from prisoner to prisoner, examining their faces. "Hopefully she's locked in one of the challenges, but we can't take that chance. Time affects that one strangely, after the incident at her birth. I'm not sure we can trust her to stay slowed down."

The two moved out of his sight, and Owen gave them a few seconds before breathing and blinking his eyes. What did they mean, the incident at Kara's birth? How did time have a weird effect on Kara? Was it that thing about paradoxes not affecting her?

Once the two agents had moved past the Countess and headed toward the challenges, Owen dropped to his knees to hide, then looked around. He let out a sigh of relief as he spied Kara under the table she'd been standing on. She was grabbing a prisoner's leg from there, looking like she was about to take a bite out of it. The idea made him almost smile as he quickly crawled over to her, wondering how he'd be able to get her out of here without the agents seeing.

He touched her hand to try to pry her fingers off the prisoner, but as soon as he made contact, Kara's mouth closed on the man's leg, and she bit down hard, then released him in disgust.

"Ugh," she said, spitting out cloth fibers. "Guy needs to bathe more."

"Kara?" Owen whispered, sitting back in surprise. As soon as his hand left hers, though, she froze in mid–disgusted face.

What was happening? Was his power somehow transferring to her? He reached out again, grabbing her hand, and she released the prisoner, still spitting.

"Kara," he repeated. "I opened the door, but it slowed down time everywhere in the prison, and then these two agents came in out of nowhere!"

Kara took this all in, nodding along. She leaned out past the table legs for a moment, then pulled back into hiding. "I see them, but they should be far enough away. You can still make it out the exit, if you go now."

Owen shook his head. "They want *you*. They think you had something to do with this. And they said something about removing the problem, so I don't know what they'll do to you if you stay."

Kara shook her head over and over. "*I'm not leaving*, Owen. I don't care what they do to me. Whatever punishment they give is better than . . . what might happen if I leave."

Owen started to say something, when both he and Kara were dragged out from under the table.

Only, instead of facing the agents, they found themselves looking up into the faces of a bald woman and a very, very angry Countess.

Turn to page 57. ⬥❯

We go forward as far as we can," Kara continued. "Right to the end. Even if the Countess can track us from here, there's no way that trail will hold up after the planet dies. We should be safe there while we figure out what to do."

Right to the *what*, now? "I hate to bring this up," Owen said, "but how exactly are we going to survive without a planet? Don't we need air or even a place to stand? Space isn't that great for survival, I've heard."

"As long as we're moving through time, we'll be fine," she said, fiddling with the symbols on the bracelet. "The device has protective qualities that keep us alive. Just make sure you don't let go, or you'll drop back into normal time." She winced. "And if that's in deep space . . . just hold tight, okay?"

"Good tip," Owen said, grabbing her hand. She smiled sadly, then hit a button on the bracelet, and the entire world jolted.

Time began moving forward rapidly all around them. Leaves on the trees vibrated in the wind, while insects and dinosaurs zoomed past them, or even sometimes right through them. Apparently time travel made you insubstantial, which was convenient for them.

For a moment Owen wondered if that was something the author of Kara's books had put into place, or whether *real* time travel actually made you ghostlike. That moment passed when he realized there wasn't any such thing as "real" time travel, so that was sort of a silly question.

"Now that we're a bit farther away, I'm going to speed us up," Kara said. She pushed a symbol on the bracelet, and time began moving even faster, with animals flashing by too quickly to see, and day and night mixing into each other.

"How did you learn how to use that thing?" Owen asked her, unable to look away from the various changes in the world around them. Different dinosaurs appeared, ones from later periods, and then disappeared just as quickly. Owen could have sworn he even saw a few furry early mammals, but they passed by too fast for him to be sure.

"My older self showed me," she said, and Owen noticed she wasn't watching the show in front of them but was instead just staring off into space. "It's not that hard, actually. The TSA made them pretty user-friendly."

"Except they're not around to make them anymore," Owen pointed out. "And wait, if your older self showed you how to use it, then how did she learn it?"

"Because I grow up and show myself," Kara said. "I know it doesn't make sense, but try not to think about it too much. Remember, paradoxes don't affect me." She squeezed his hand. "Just part of my charm."

He smiled at that and realized that in spite of only knowing her for a few hours, that's not how it felt for some reason. It *was* almost like he'd known her for longer. Maybe not a year, like she claimed, but certainly for days at least.

Though that made sense, if they'd had to do all three challenges to get the exit code for the readers. Owen briefly wondered what he'd found out about Kara in that time. Had she shared what this terrible future thing she was going to do was? Or anything about this whole "immune to paradoxes" thing, which still made no sense? Paradoxes weren't like the TSA agents, police that punished you for breaking a rule. They were impossibilities of logic, a broken series of events that shouldn't and couldn't actually happen in the way that they did. How could an impossibility *not* affect Kara?

Yet here they were, using a TSA time bracelet that shouldn't exist, that Kara's older self had taught her younger self to use, only so she could grow up and teach her younger self again. It was a circle in time with no beginning.

"You're thinking about it," Kara said. "I can hear your teeth grinding."

"Fair enough," he told her, trying to unclench his teeth but failing. At that moment a bright light filled the sky, surprising Owen to the point he almost lost his grip on Kara's hand. She squeezed his hand automatically, as if making sure he didn't go anywhere as she glanced at her bracelet.

"That would be the meteor that killed off the dinosaurs," she said, then turned her head up to the sky. "And here I was hoping that it'd been aliens, preparing the world for humanity. Guess that means humans weren't brought here from another planet!"

Owen's eyes widened. "Is that . . . something people were worried about?"

She grinned at him, appearing to mean it this time. "I love how gullible you are. It just brings me joy."

The dinosaurs were now completely gone, and ice passed

through Owen and Kara like waves on the ocean, forming and melting with the changing seasons almost like breathing. Then abruptly the ice pulled away, migrating back in what Owen assumed was a northern direction. Or was it south? It's not like he had any idea where they were in the world. Really, the time prison could have been anywhere.

Mammals began running past and through them now, with new species appearing almost every second. "Are we close to human civilization?" Owen asked.

Kara checked the bracelet. "Still a few million years short. You'll have to watch for it, 'cause it does fly by."

"What do you mean, 'fly by'?" he asked, his blood running cold. "Do we not have long? Does another meteor come? What *happens*?"

She grinned at him again, and the smile seemed to come more easily. "You never learn, do you?"

"Ha-ha," he said, glaring at her. Still, why had he been so worried? This wasn't the nonfictional world, it was a book. The future here wasn't *his* future.

Though it might be, if he didn't find a way back to Bethany.

A few Neanderthals showed up for the briefest of instances before disappearing, replaced by very early human beings.

Those humans advanced quickly from primitive tools to spears and onward, and soon canvas dwellings began to spring up that looked familiar. Were those Native Americans? Apparently they *had* been in North America all along.

Not long after that a wagon train zoomed by, and soon roads sprang up all around them, and eventually, so did wooden signposts. The signs didn't last long at first, but after turning to metal, they stayed in place long enough to read.

"Mount Rushmore?" Owen said, pointing at the closest sign as time flew by. Apparently they were in South Dakota, and far off in the distance the mountain monument rose into the air.

"Coming up on the twenty-first century," Kara said as she fiddled with the bracelet's speed. The world around them began to slow down a bit, now only moving a few months or so a second instead of years, decades, or centuries.

"Shouldn't we stop here?" Owen asked, turning away from the view. This was where he needed to be, after all. Or maybe a few days earlier, so he could rescue Bethany before she was even in danger. That would be perfect, and make him feel much less guilty about how much time he'd potentially wasted getting out of the time prison!

"I don't know that it's safe," Kara said, giving him a worried look. "The Countess would come looking for us here first, since she must know this is my proper time. We should probably make sure we've lost her by passing our time, then turning around and coming back from the future. That way we'll see any trap after it's sprung and be able to deal with it."

Owen nodded, trying not to think too hard about the logic of what she'd just said. Mostly, he just wanted to jump off the time travel ride in the present and get on with finding his friend. *Bethany, I hope you're okay . . .*

Kara clicked the symbols on her bracelet, and they began to slide forward faster again, a few years at a time . . . only for Kara to abruptly smack the bracelet hard, immediately dropping them back into normal time. The time travel stopped so quickly, Owen almost felt whiplash, even though they hadn't actually been moving at all.

"What's wrong?" he asked, shaking off the confusion.

Kara didn't speak, but dropped his hand and took a step forward, staring into the distance. Owen moved to follow, then looked up to see what she was looking at.

Mount Rushmore.

All four heads were the Countess.

Kara strode in silence to the sign marking the entrance to

the park. "'In honor of our Supreme Queen,'" she read.

Owen moved up beside her and continued reading. "'May her enemies suffer eternal punishment for their crimes.'"

"So, um, right," Kara said, turning to look at him with panic spreading over her face. "We *might* have a problem."

NO, THIS IS TOO MUCH OF A CLICHÉ. LET'S FORGET ABOUT THIS AND GO BACK TO THE BEGINNING OF TIME INSTEAD.

Turn to page 341. ⬍〉

LET'S FIND OUT HOW THIS HAPPENED!

Turn to page 296. ⬍〉

Ⓘf we can find some way across this ravine, we might be safe on the other side," Kara said, pointing over the yawning abyss before them. "It's too far to jump, but these trees look springy enough that we might be able to cross by bending them."

Okay, right. Because bending trees over a ravine never went wrong. Still, the ground was shaking with T. rex footfalls again, so it must have finished off the other dinosaur.

Either that, or they were teaming up.

"Trees it is!" Owen said, pulling Kara to the nearest one. The trunk was ridged in a way that provided easy hand- and foot-holds, which helped, considering they'd have to hold hands the entire way. Even still, the climb took way too long, considering what was rumbling toward them.

Around ten feet up, the tree began to bend out over the ravine, and they quickened their climb, even as Owen tried to ignore how much nothingness was below them now. The ravine was so dark, there was no way to see the bottom, but what he could see would already be way too long a fall. It wouldn't take much to send them plummeting, either; the tree's springiness made them pretty unstable even when the shaking ground wasn't bouncing the tree. At least the T. rex hadn't arrived yet—

The monster exploded into view and let out an enormous roar as it located its prey. Owen shouted in warning, and they began sidling forward on the tree as it bent horizontally out over the ravine. If this could be timed right, maybe they could drop off the tree onto the other side, then let it spring back up and hit the T. rex's face? Cartoons did that sort of thing often enough, so how hard could it be?

Except as Owen got closer to the top of the tree, the trunk began dropping even farther, quickly falling almost past the edge of the ravine. And that's when he realized they'd made a *really* unfortunate mistake: This particular tree wasn't tall enough to make it to the other side.

"We're going to have to jump!" he told Kara. "Can you stand?"

"I think so," she said, and tried to push to her feet.

But it was already too late. The T. rex roared again, then came crashing straight for them, plowing into the trunk. The tree yanked out of the ground entirely and tumbled straight into the ravine, with the dinosaur right behind it.

Owen's heart began beating crazily as he, Kara, the tree, and the dinosaur all fell. Everything around him slowed, and he wondered if this was what dying was like. Was his entire life going to flash before his eyes, or just the worst parts? And would those parts be an endless repeat of him picking the wrong tree?

"Are you doing this?" Kara asked him at normal speed, and Owen realized it wasn't just him that had slowed down. Wait, *had* he done this, sped up their time even more? He put his hand over his heart and gasped; it was beating so fast it felt like one solid buzzing, like a hummingbird's wings. This must be adrenaline or something kicking in. Good thing his heart was robotic, because there was no way a normal heart could have taken this!

Time slowed even more, and the T. rex froze in midair, as did the tree. Spots began to pop in Owen's sight, and darkness started creeping in around the edges of his vision, but at least they'd stopped falling.

Kara helped Owen to his feet on the tree trunk, which felt as solid as a rock below them now, in the slowed time. Together, they waited for the top of the tree to fall just short of the other side, which as fast as it was going in real time, still just took a few seconds. That was good, because Owen wasn't sure how much longer he could keep this going.

"Now!" Kara shouted, and half pulled, half led Owen in a run toward the end of the trunk. Just as they reached the giant palm fronds jutting out of the tree, they both leaped as far as they could, off into nothingness.

Owen slammed into the side of the ravine at his chest, and the impact forced Kara's hand from his. He frantically grabbed at the edge to keep from falling backward as a wave of dizziness passed over him and weakness took his arms. But somehow he managed to grab ahold of a root, slowing himself enough to at least see that Kara had made it okay. In fact, she looked fine in every way except that she was floating in midair, frozen in time.

The dizziness got worse, and it felt like the ravine was moving beneath him as the root slipped in his hand. "Help?" Owen said quietly, reaching out for another handhold, anything that could help him up over the edge. But there was nothing. His vision grew even darker, and he suddenly couldn't stay awake, no matter how hard he tried. Everything went black . . .

From a distance, he felt something grab his arm. "Owen!" someone shouted from miles away, and then dragged him up and over onto the other side. A sharp slap struck his cheek, and the darkness opened enough for Owen to make out Kara's terrified face.

"Hello?" he said.

"Are you okay?" she shouted, then gently patted his cheek a few times. "Owen? Stay with me. You almost fell!"

This seemed *odd*. Hadn't she been frozen a moment ago? "How did . . ."

"I think your power gave out," she said. "We're both moving at normal speed again. Listen."

He concentrated hard and heard nothing but the buzzing squeaks and short blips he'd heard back in the air lock. Fear took over, and he struggled to sit up. "The dinosaur—"

"He's at the bottom of the ravine," Kara said, glancing past Owen. "The tree, too, I assume. But we made it. And nothing's attacked us over here, so I'm hoping we're safe!" She hugged him tightly, and he weakly patted her with one hand before his strength gave out and it dropped back to the ground.

"So . . . tired," he told her. "Very, very."

"I know," she said, and smiled gently. "You sleep, okay? I'll watch over you."

He nodded at that, barely able to even think anymore. "I sleep."

And with that, he did.

What could have been hours or days later, Owen opened his eyes to what looked like a full moon and stars in the sky. He immediately sat up, his entire body crying out in pain, like he'd run a marathon or something. "Kara?" he said.

"Right here," came a voice from behind him, and Owen twisted to find Kara lying on the ground as well, staring up at the stars. "I was just about to try to wake you, actually. It's got to be close to midnight."

Owen let out a relieved breath, then looked all around them. "So no more dinosaurs?"

"Nope, all clear," Kara told him. "I guess the prison designers figured that if you can get this far, why not give you a break?"

"What about the exit code?" Owen asked. "Did you find it anywhere?"

Kara turned over and smiled at him. "Look up."

Owen frowned but turned his gaze to the sky. "What, the moon?"

Kara crawled over next to him, then grabbed his head and turned it slightly, aiming his gaze toward the stars to the left of the moon. "They did a great job making this look like the outside world," Kara said. "But I'm pretty sure I've never seen a constellation like that."

Right over the spot where the air lock was, Owen saw an enormous numeral "2" made out of stars.

Above. The. Air lock. Were they kidding?! "We could have stayed in the air lock until dark, then come out just long enough to see it!" he shouted, then winced in pain as his body screamed back at him. "Was this all just to torture us?"

"We'd never have known it was there," Kara said. "And honestly, I bet you can't see it unless you're pretty far out here anyway. Plus, you'd still have to be able to survive outside long enough to find it."

That was true. "Still, though. We almost got eaten by dinosaurs, all just for a big number two." He looked around in the darkness. "At least we don't have to go back. I'm not sure I've got it in me for a return trip anyway."

She nodded. "Just don't forget to use whatever nonfictional trick you're going to do, so we remember the code."

Right! Owen concentrated hard. *Don't forget, readers. The*

first digit is two. Write it down or something. Two is the first num-
ber in the exit code. Two is—

And then midnight hit, and everything reversed a day.

**Turn back to page 1 . . . or cheat a bit
and skip ahead to the decisions on
page 259.**

Branson in the year fourteen," Kara said, grabbing Owen's hand and hitting the bracelet.

They jumped forward in time, landing in the middle of several wooden huts, each about ten feet tall, arranged in a circle around a central open area. Though no one saw them appear, Owen could hear voices just on the other side of one of the structures.

"This might be a bit early for the founding of the TSA," Owen pointed out.

"That's the thing, though," Kara said. "The founder could have traveled to the past in order to stay safe. Anyway, it was just the time and place that popped into my head. Should we try something else?"

"No need," said a voice, and they whirled around to find Dolores with several robed guards. She immediately touched

Owen and Kara on the neck, and they both collapsed to the ground.

The last thing Owen heard was Dolores's voice getting farther and farther away. "Bring them, but keep them asleep. The Countess doesn't want them to wake up before she disposes of them."

Readers, turn back now! This is the . . . the wrong . . .

And then everything went dark.

*T*HIS IS MESSED UP. DON'T SPLIT BETHANY, NOBODY. LET THESE TWO GO.

The thoughts echoed in Owen's head, but without the force of a command. This was more like readers were speaking through him. He immediately opened his mouth to share the news with Nobody. "They said—"

"Oh, I heard," Nobody said, his hands still raised over Bethany.

Owen let out the biggest sigh of relief, almost falling over onto his face.

"However," Nobody said, "this isn't your story, it's *mine*. And it appears that the readers need a lesson in how an author actually controls everything."

"What?!" Owen shouted. "You promised!"

"Did you really think I'd allow someone to change *my* story?"

Nobody asked him. "This was a Pick the Plot book, yes. But there was only ever one path through, and it led straight here to me. I couldn't just leave things to chance, now could I, Owen?" He moved his hands from above Bethany's head to place them on both sides of her face, then shook his head. "Apologies if this hurts," he said to her.

"No!" Doc Twilight screamed again, but it was too late. Nobody tore his hands apart, and Bethany split with a sound like a book being torn in half. Two Bethanys fell to the ground, each one looking like a whole person but somehow . . . not. Each one looked a bit dimmer than before, as if neither one was fully there.

"Bethany!" Owen screamed, and tried to push forward, but Fowen yanked his chains backward, pulling Owen to the floor.

"And now, the last portal," Nobody said, opening another page in reality. Behind it lay a night sky, with stars shining over a pirate ship and a beautiful-looking island. Nobody pointed at one of the stars, then moved his finger to the next star to the left. "There we go, the second star from the right," he said, then picked up one of the Bethanys. "And home you go!"

And with that, the featureless man tossed Bethany up

through the page, into the night sky above the island, and straight at the star.

"You'll kill her!" Owen shouted.

"Actually, I'm returning her to the nonfictional world," Nobody said. "The portal to Neverland is the last one remaining open." On the other side of the page, Bethany sailed toward the star only to abruptly disappear. "And there she goes."

Owen couldn't speak. There was nothing to say. Above him Doc Twilight moaned, and Owen could hear the sizzle of tears hitting the molten plastic.

"You've disappointed me, readers," Nobody said to no one in particular. "Did you not see throughout this book that you were being taught a lesson as well?" His face grew a frown. "I hoped better of you, especially here, at the end. It can't be helped, I suppose."

"Don't blame them for your lies," Owen hissed.

Nobody paused. "You know, I did intend to leave you here in the fictional world as a gift, Owen. Reunite you with Kara and let you live out your proper story with her. You would have lived an eventful, adventurous life with her. But now I believe I'll instead sentence you to your well-deserved nonfictional life."

One of his enormous arms snaked out and grabbed Owen, cutting through the chains holding him. As Owen struggled, Nobody pulled him up toward the rip in reality. "Good luck," the featureless man said, then threw Owen directly at the same star he'd sent Bethany toward.

Owen screamed as he soared out into empty night air, passing over the pirate ship anchored nearby a skull rock. Somehow, gravity wasn't yanking him down, but that didn't stop him from almost dying of fright.

The ship and island disappeared in the darkness, and for a few moments Owen couldn't see anything but stars. He wondered if Nobody had thrown him out into space, but there was still air to breathe here.

And then something buzzed over his skin like he was passing through some kind of energy field, and suddenly, lights appeared out of nowhere below him. Lights from a city. A giant city.

"And now," said Nobody's voice from a great distance, "I close the last portal."

Something ripped in space behind him, and Owen instantly began to tumble down toward the city, falling faster and faster as he went. Gravity seemed to have caught up to him now.

The weird thing was, Owen wasn't afraid anymore, not even while tumbling to his certain death. It was as if all fear had just disappeared. Instead, he watched the ground rising toward him very matter-of-factly, counting down the seconds it would take until he hit.

But just before he crashed into a city street, some unknown force that felt very similar to the Magister's magic grabbed Owen, slowing him down and carrying him into the open window of a large mansion within the city. That same force set him down on a very old bed in the middle of what looked like an abandoned nursery. Nearby, Bethany lay on another bed unconscious.

Owen slowly sat up and examined his surroundings. Somehow, he felt an odd ache in his mind, as if there was something missing . . . something that both asked and answered questions, questions like where he was and how he'd come from the second star on the right to what looked like present-day London. Questions of how he would get home, or what would happen to him and Bethany in a newly separated nonfictional world.

Fortunately, though, the ache was easily ignored. Owen pushed himself off the bed, checked to make sure Bethany was alive, then set out to find a phone. He'd have to call his mother to arrange for transportation, and then perhaps find something to eat.

It was the only logical thing to do.

THE END

I'm not thrilled with you, readers. But join me for Story Thieves: *Worlds Apart*, to see the new world of possibility and freedom you actively chose against. Perhaps you will learn the lesson I so fervently wished you to learn in this book.

First, there was nothing.

And then, there was light, light so bright that Owen had to cover his eyes with his arm.

Was he dead? Should he be heading toward the light somehow?

But the light dimmed as his vision adjusted, and he slowly opened his eyes to find himself lying on solid ground. Not only that, but time was moving forward again, as far as he could tell. At least, he could feel a breeze, and see weirdly vibrant trees of all varieties blowing with the wind. And the air! It almost had a taste to it, it was so pure and refreshing.

Owen pushed himself up on his forearms, then glanced down to see that he was lying on brightly colored warm tiles. The tiles had been decorated so intricately that for a moment, Owen was mesmerized by the pattern, and he had to purposely look away just to keep from getting lost in it. Nearby, ocean waves surged onto sand of different colors, including reds, blues, and even black. Between the ocean and the bright sun, this all looked like a vacation postcard, just from a planet more beautiful than his own.

Was this . . . heaven?

Something stirred to his right, and Owen glanced over to find Kara waking up, still holding his hand. He released her gently and tried to shake off the cloudiness in his head. Where *were* they? Shouldn't they have been sucked into the big bang? *Had* they been killed by it? Or did Kara manage to jump them over the nothingness and into . . . well, whatever had come before the beginning of the universe?

If this was a previous universe, Owen decided he wouldn't necessarily mind staying.

"Wow," Kara said, sitting up and looking around. "Can't say I saw *this* coming."

"You don't think we died, do you?" Owen whispered.

She grinned at him, then threw her arms around his shoulders and hugged him. "Nope, I think we're both still pretty alive," she said, putting her ear to his chest. "See? I can hear your heart beating. That same weird metallic thump as usual."

Blushing as bright as the sun, Owen wriggled his way out of her grasp and pushed himself to his feet, wavering a bit as a bout of dizziness passed over him. He turned away from the ocean and steadied himself, then noticed what lay behind them.

Buildings thousands of feet tall and made of colored light swirled up into the sky, each one more beautiful and less possible than the last. It was as if builders had managed to construct them of rainbows. Every building was a piece of art, and yet stood so tall and strong that they could have been sculpted from stone or steel.

"Where *are* we?" Owen whispered to Kara, who stood beside him, her mouth hanging open.

"I really wish I knew," she said. "This must be whatever came before our universe. Remember what I said, about how there are theories that societies millions of years more advanced than ours might have the power to build their own universe?" She nodded at the city before them. "This might be one of those."

That idea made Owen's head hurt, but also brought up a thousand more questions. Was *this* still part of the Kara Dox books? Or had they somehow gone beyond the fictional universe itself? Either way, what did this mean? And most important, could they get back?

"We can always ask someone where we are," Kara said, pointing at the buildings. Owen looked closer, and realized that there were people walking between them . . . and not just at ground level. Some crossed on bridges at incredible heights, while others . . .

Others were floating through the air. They were *flying*.

"Maybe we should fix your time bracelet first," Owen said, his excitement matching his terror at the scene before him. If these people could actually fly, then how advanced were they? What else could they do? And were they friendly?

Kara nodded, then looked down at her wrist and frowned. "Huh. Slight problem." She held it up for Owen to see.

The time bracelet had cracked completely in half.

Owen's entire body went rigid. "Tell me you can still fix this," he said slowly. "Tell me we're not going to be stuck here in this time."

"There's always a chance I can salvage it," Kara said, then gently touched the bracelet.

It immediately cracked again, into four separate pieces, then fell to the ground.

"Hmm," Kara said. "Maybe not a *big* chance—"

The pieces began to smoke before bursting into flames.

"Yeah, we're not going anywhere," Kara said, giving Owen a guilty look. "Not yet, anyway. But I *will* find a way to get you back to the present. Maybe the floating people can help us?"

Owen turned away, unable to respond. Had the readers done this to him? Purposely sent him here so there was no way he could ever get back and find Bethany? Who would do such a thing? And if they had, how could he fight it? He couldn't control the story, not like the readers could. It was like Nobody had thrown him into a river, and every time he thought he could reach the shore, the readers added a waterfall. And now he was about to drown.

Owen walked toward the ocean, trying not to think about the majestic city behind him where he might be spending the rest of his life. He stared out into the deeply blue water, noticing absently how beautiful it was, especially compared to the ocean back home. The air seemed to shimmer above the water a few hundred feet out from shore, and Owen wondered what that could be. Maybe some sort of protective wall or force field? He wasn't sure if that made him feel more safe, or more trapped.

"I'm so sorry, Owen," Kara said, moving to his side and staring out at the ocean as well. "I never would have sent us back if I had any . . ." She trailed off as she seemed to notice something. "Hey, are those boats?"

It took Owen a few seconds to realize she was asking him a question. "Boats? Where?"

She pointed off to the left, and Owen's eyes widened.

Sailing toward shore from outside the shimmering light were more boats than Owen could even count. They extended off into the distance beyond what he could see, and they were coming in fast.

Something launched from one of the boats and sailed out toward the city, only to collide with the shimmering air and explode, sending light sizzling off in all directions. So it *was* some sort of force field.

"We should get off the beach," Owen said, and Kara nodded. Before they could move, though, an odd, musical alarm erupted behind them in the city, and very human-looking people floated out of the buildings, each one wearing elaborate robes. Even from this distance Owen could tell that the humans seemed far too old and fragile to still be alive, let alone up and moving, while also carrying staffs or books . . .

Wait a second. Were these . . . magicians? And here he was, completely Kiel-less, without even a winged cat or spell book. Charm would so be laughing at him right now . . .

"You know, if this right now is some sort of final battle that ends their universe, we might have a problem," Kara said, looking up to watch as the elderly city protectors floated over their heads toward the sea.

"*A* problem?"

"What happens if we interfere?" she said quietly. "If we mess something up, we might stop our universe from being created. We could be dooming everyone who's ever lived. If it comes to a choice about whether or not we get involved—"

"It's not a choice!" Owen said quickly, hopefully interrupting the readers before they decided anything. The last thing he needed was to give the readers the power to determine if Kara's entire universe existed or not! "You're totally right, we can't get in the way. Whatever happens here needs to happen exactly the way it always did."

"But what if they need our help?" Kara said, pointing at the apparent-wizards assembling just before the shimmering light out over the water. More shots rang out from the boats, hitting the protective wall in multiple places, and each one sent the same sparks sizzling away. More and more of the boats approached, starting to fill the horizon.

"I think they've got this in hand," Owen told her. "Look at them. They're floating and they have a magical wall. What could possibly hurt them?"

Something crackled loudly farther out than Owen could see, and an arc of lightning pulsed right through the shimmering light. It struck one of the floating humans in the chest, sending her flying backward to crash into the tile just feet from Owen and Kara, hitting so hard she left a smoking hole a few feet deep. Before they could even react, though, the woman stood up, looking merely dazed, and floated out of the hole. Considering she had to be over two hundred years old, Owen couldn't help but be impressed.

"Are you okay?" Kara shouted, running over to her.

The woman looked them over with surprise, then waved her staff. Both Kara and Owen lit up briefly, and the woman sighed in what sounded like relief. "You're not Naturalists, thank the source." She paused, looking closer. "But you're not from here, either. Who *are* you?"

Kara glanced at Owen, then shrugged as if to say, *What choice do we have?* "We're from the future. We came back by accident, but don't know where we are or what's happening. Can we help in some way?"

The woman sagged, putting most of her weight on her staff. "I'm afraid not, child. I fear you've arrived just in time to witness the last days of Atlantis, as well as of all magic on Earth. The unbelievers have arrived in force to wipe us out, and they may have the power to do just that."

Owen took a step back, feeling like he'd just been smacked in the face. He shook his head, unable to wrap his mind around what the woman had just said. This was Earth? Or some version of it? And the city behind them was *Atlantis*? But how could that be possible? They'd gone back beyond the big bang, so how could there even be an Earth? Did the universes just repeat themselves somehow and create the same planets over and over? If that was the case, why was this Atlantis still around at the end of their universe, when all of the legends of the city had placed it in the distant past on Owen's Earth?

The woman, meanwhile, was staring at Owen intently. "You're from the future, you say?" She took a step closer and touched her staff to his head. He glowed briefly again, and her eyes widened. She touched Kara as well, but this time frowned and turned back to Owen. "Come, I must bring you to the council. They must see for themselves what the future holds."

Owen looked at Kara, who winced. "We really need to find a way back home," Owen told the woman, backing away slowly. "The future doesn't really wait for anyone. It's a huge pain like that. And you seem to have a lot going on here—"

"I'm afraid I must insist," the woman said, and raised her staff.

MAKE OWEN FIGHT THE WOMAN!

Turn to page—

The woman tilted her head, giving Owen a strange look. "I see we have witnesses," she said, then began murmuring something while moving her staff around both him and Kara. Finally, she nodded. "You are free of their influence now, unless you grant them control again. Now, enough of this. We must be off."

Again, Owen felt like he'd been hit. Witnesses? She couldn't have seen the *readers*, could she? They did have influence over him, obviously, but how could she have taken that away, let alone even known they were there?

And if she could stop the readers from changing the very story they were in . . . what did she have the power to do to him and Kara?

~~WAIT, WHAT HAPPENED? SHE CAN'T~~

~~STOP US FROM DECIDING THINGS.~~

~~OWEN HAS TO LISTEN TO US.~~

~~Turn to page ███.~~ ⬍❯

LOOKS LIKE WE DON'T HAVE A CHOICE. JUST GO ALONG WITH IT.

Turn to page 93. ⬍❯

I assume you brought me the time travel device?" Nobody said, his featureless head looking around for it as his enormous arms held a struggling Owen off the ground.

Owen didn't answer, and Nobody's grip tightened, forcing a groan out of him. "No!" he said finally.

"Yes, you did," Nobody said, and squeezed again. "Why do you think I put you in that story? There's no way Kara would have let you come here alone."

"That's true," Kara said from above as she dropped feet-first onto Nobody's head. The force of the blow split Nobody into two, but each half just re-formed after she passed. Kara looked shocked but quickly slapped her bracelet before crashing into the ground, only to reappear behind him, sweeping her leg into his. His body morphed around her leg, then quickly solidified, holding her in place as another arm appeared out of his chest, grabbing the time bracelet from her wrist.

"Thank you," he said, dropping her to the ground. "You are free to go, Kara Dox. I wish you well, as I do all fictionals." Another arm appeared out of his side and ripped open a page back to her world right in the middle of the factory.

"What? No!" she screamed as the Magister murmured something, and Kara rose up off the floor. "Put me down! Owen, I'll find a way back, I swear! I won't leave you here! This can't be happening again. Not *again*—"

And then the Magister's magic floated her through the ripped page, and it closed behind her. Just like that, Kara was gone.

"Poor girl," Nobody said, his extra arms melting back into his body as he resumed a more human shape. "I regret putting her through all of this, but hopefully she learned what your readers did: All of this is the fault of the nonfictionals."

Owen struck out in every direction, his anger pounding in his head, but Nobody's arms just moved with him, keeping him from gaining any purchase. "It's not the nonfictionals!" Owen shouted. "This is all *your* fault. You did this! You put me in a story and gave readers control, but it was all for your gain, wasn't it? You just wanted Kara's time bracelet! You played the fictional readers just as much as you say nonfictional authors do!"

Nobody slowly brought Owen up to his featureless face and stared at him with empty eye sockets. "Don't you think I could have retrieved this device myself if I wanted to?" he asked softly. "Or had the Magister use his magic to accomplish the same thing? This was about offering my people justice for a lifetime spent under your people's thumbs. The fact that it also aided me was secondary." A mouth appeared, and it smiled. "Not that I didn't enjoy it a bit myself."

"What are you going to do with Kara's bracelet?" Owen demanded.

Nobody set him down on the floor right in front of Fowen, who quickly wrapped some factory chains around his arms. "I'm going to retrieve Bethany and remove her powers permanently by splitting her in two. Why, did you think my plans would have changed at some point?"

"No, you monster!" Doc Twilight screamed from above the molten plastic. He momentarily freed his arms and started to aim his twilight launcher, only for the chains to snake around him once more. He struggled even harder, but the chains dropped him several feet closer to the molten plastic and he went still.

"I won't hurt you if you cooperate, Christian," Nobody said. "But try to escape again, and my magical associate will drop you."

"We could make the biggest Doc Twilight action figure ever," Fowen said, then winked at Owen, who tried hard not to throw up in his mouth. How could his fictional self be so different from him? There must be something to this whole evil twin thing.

The Magister stepped near Nobody and took one of the man's featureless hands, then magically floated the machine Fowen had stolen into his arms. Nobody nodded at him, then pushed some buttons on the time bracelet, and they both disappeared.

Before either Owen or Doc Twilight could even try to free themselves, they reappeared, the machine now buzzing loudly and shaking slightly, glowing with some kind of bright light.

"What is that thing?" Owen asked.

"You missed all the good stuff," Fowen told him. "Bethany turned into a beam of light to stop the Dark, but then she went sailing off like light does. Doc Twilight and his sidekick found some old supervillain machine that vacuums up light and tried to save her with it. Only by that point, she was too far away. Light moves pretty fast, after all."

"*Must you* explain the plan to him?" Nobody asked. "We

really should rise above the temptation for that sort of thing." His face turned toward Owen. "Still, there's nothing he can do, so I suppose it doesn't hurt."

"That's where the time bracelet came in," Fowen continued, like Nobody hadn't interrupted. "All we had to do was go back to the moment Bethany hit the Dark, then turn the machine on. It could then vacuum up all of the light including her, but with everything going on right then, I'm sure no one noticed a quick flash of darkness. Especially since the light came back as soon as they captured her and turned the machine off. And now—"

"And now, the Magister will find Bethany for us," Nobody said, and placed the machine in the middle of the factory floor.

The magician began to murmur a spell, and the machine buzzed louder and louder. Lights of all different colors exploded out, searing Owen's eyes with their brightness, but he couldn't look away. Faster and faster the light emerged, and the machine's noise grew overpowering, to the point that Owen couldn't hear anything else.

And then the machine went quiet, expelling one final beam of light, which froze in midair, unlike the rest. The Magister moved his hands in a circular fashion, and the light began to spin, faster and faster until it was moving so quickly in such a particular pattern that it began to take on the shape of a human being. A girl.

"Do it," Nobody said, and the Magister nodded, changing his chanting.

The light solidified, taking on colors and dimensions. Hair turned reddish bronze, and clothes emerged from the brightness, followed by a face. And then before Owen knew it, Bethany was there, floating before them with her eyes closed as she spun around.

"Please," Doc Twilight said, his voice breaking. "Don't do this."

"I must, Christian," Nobody told him. "You know I must." He stepped over to Bethany and raised both of his hands.

Owen squirmed in his chains, knowing he had to do something, *anything*. But what could he do? There was no way he could defeat even the Magister, let alone Nobody, too. And Fowen wasn't going to help. Kara wouldn't have a way to get back to this story, if she even knew where it was. And he couldn't move to open a page to her story, or anyone else's. Besides, Nobody could just close it instantly.

But there had to be *something*! Maybe he could convince Nobody how wrong this was? Not that there was any way

Nobody would ever listen to a nonfictional person.

But to a fictional person? One who knew the whole story?

"Wait!" Owen shouted. "I have a deal for you!"

Nobody's hands paused just over Bethany's head. "I have no interest in your schemes, Owen. This must be done."

"This isn't about me," he said. "This is about whether or not *fictional* people think you're right to do this."

Nobody turned his head back to Owen without moving his body. "If they don't, that just means they haven't yet learned the truth."

"I know a bunch who've heard your truth," Owen said. "Why not ask the readers of this book if they agree with you?"

Nobody slowly grew a face and used it to stare at Owen. "What game are you playing, boy?"

"Just this," Owen said, hoping this would work. "You're convinced that you're helping fictional people. But maybe they don't all think your way is the only way. Or even right to begin with. Why not ask them? If the readers think you're right, then you can do whatever it is you're about to do to Bethany and separate the worlds. But if they think you're *wrong*, you let us all go and promise to leave Bethany alone for the rest of her life."

Nobody slowly smiled. "Letting the readers pick the plot,

eh, Owen? Very well, I accept your bargain. We shall let the readers decide."

Owen nodded and closed his eyes. *Readers. I really hope you can still hear me. You've been in control of what happens in this book, I know. And at first, I hated that, just like you probably hated nonfictional authors supposedly doing it to you. But after everything I've seen, I don't believe that anymore. Authors don't have any more control over the fictional world than they do over their own lives.*

So much of the time, we think we have no control. Our parents make choices for us, or our teachers. We get angry about it, just wanting to make our own decisions, and dream about being adults so we're totally in control. But they're just as powerless as we are, a lot of the time. Because other people are making choices around you too, and sometimes that means things don't go your way. Or sometimes things just spin away from you, whether it's bad luck or something you didn't see coming. People get sick, or our friends move away, and it's horrible, and we feel like we just want to tell everyone to stay exactly where they are, because that's what we *want.*

They never listen.

Controlling someone else is always wrong. We all know that. But sometimes you have to trust in other people and let them make decisions that might go really badly for you, because you don't have the power to make those choices yourself. And that's what I'm doing now.

I can't decide for you if nonfictional authors have control over you or not. I've lived out Kiel Gnomenfoot's life for a bit, and Jonathan Porterhouse definitely didn't tell me what to do. And even when you readers tried to make me do things, I still had a choice. Maybe it's different because I'm nonfictional, but I doubt it.

I don't know who's right or wrong here. But I do know that at this moment, you're *in control. You get to decide if an innocent girl is split in two, and if Nobody puts the worlds at risk by splitting them. We know what's happening in Kara's future. What if splitting the worlds caused that?*

All I can do is ask you to please, please *help us. Help Bethany. And help your world too. It's all up to you now.*

DO YOU DECIDE TO HELP BETHANY AND OWEN?

Turn to page 224. ⬥❯

DO YOU DECIDE THAT NOBODY IS RIGHT, AND THE WORLDS NEED TO SPLIT?

Turn to page 309. ⬥❯

ATTACK! IT'S YOUR ONLY CHANCE!

Adrenaline coursed through Owen's body as the thought hit his brain, and he threw himself at the woman with all of his strength. "Run, Kara!" he shouted, knocking the woman to the ground, his robotic heart beating hard against his chest. He landed on top of the woman and rolled off . . . only to feel a cold chill pass through his body as her hand touched his arm.

"Just for that, you little runt, I hope you *enjoy* this," the woman said, sneering down at him as Owen's muscles began to seize up, jerking his arms and legs painfully toward his body.

He tried to yell for help, but all that came out was a low moan. A few teeth fell out of his mouth, and he looked down at them in shock, only to find his hands had shriveled up into claws. His skin looked practically transparent now, and his arms began to shake with the effort of holding himself up.

"Owen!" Kara shouted from his side, sounding panicked as she reached down and turned his head toward her. "I'll fix this, okay? *I promise.* Don't worry. I'll make this right." She gripped his arm tightly enough to cause him pain, then seemed to whisper something over and over that sounded like "Not again. *Not again.*"

"How will you make it right when you're dust, my dear Kara?" the woman asked as everything began to blur in Owen's vision. He tried speaking again, but now even breathing was difficult. It was like he'd aged a hundred years in a matter of seconds.

Someone shouted something from far away, but even thinking was too hard at this point. He just needed to sleep. That was it. Sleep.

Ah, readers. You have apparently aged Owen to death. Fortunately, everything resets at the end of the day, so turn back to page 1 (or cheat and turn to page 103) and try not to let him die quite so quickly next time?

Kara led Owen away from the Countess, down the hallway full of cells, and out into a large circular room that looked a thousand feet wide. Four hallways just like the one they'd come from led out of the room like spokes on a wheel, while three large air locks sat in between the hallways. The wall across from the air locks held an enormous door, probably the exit.

Tables filled the center of the room, piled high with the most amazing food Owen had seen in his life. The nearest tables were covered in various breakfast foods, from pancakes two inches thick to muffins as large as his head, covered in icing. Everything seemed to be heated or cooled from the table itself, which looked pretty futuristic. That made sense, since it wasn't like they had the technology to build a time prison in his present day.

Kara pulled Owen over to one side, looking worried. "I don't like this. I turned myself in to the Time Security Agency so that . . . certain things wouldn't happen in the future. But if I leave, then that will all have been pointless, and the bad things will happen again. And the Countess seems pretty sure that I *do* get out."

What could be so awful that she was willing to put herself in a time prison for the rest of eternity, just to make sure it never happened? "Maybe you do stop her, but come back?" Owen suggested. "You know, like you're out on parole, and then you give yourself up again."

Kara nodded absently, then without a word, slammed her fist right into the nearest wall. She immediately gasped in pain and slid to the ground, holding her hand carefully in her lap.

"Uh, are you okay?" he asked.

"Not even a little bit," she told him. "But we're not going to talk about it here."

Owen noticed a few of the prisoners watching from nearby, which wasn't good. The last thing they needed was to attract attention, especially if the Countess might not be the only one who knew Kara and wanted some revenge. He turned his back to them, trying to block their sight of Kara, then kneeled down in front of her. "If you think you're going to do something bad in the future, well, just don't do it? You can always change the future. That's why it's not called the past."

She looked up at him and tried to force a smile, but failed. "Maybe you're right," she said, obviously not believing it. "Sorry. This is the wrong time to be complaining anyway. We have to get *you* out of here and back to doing whatever it is that Nobody threw you in here for."

She gave him her noninjured hand and he helped her back up. She took a deep breath, still cradling her hand, then let it out. This was as good a time as any, he decided.

"How much do you know about Nobody?" he asked her.

This time she smiled for real. "A lot more than you wanted me to," she said. "But that can wait too. For now, we should eat."

Eating? That was the last thing on his mind. Though to be fair, Owen's stomach did rumble at the mention, and he glanced around at the tables piled with deliciousness. "It does smell pretty good in here."

"There's a lot of breakfast food," Kara said. "I hope everyone here likes that kind of thing. Could you imagine an eternity with food you hate?"

"Over there," Owen said, pointing to a second set of tables covered in steaming meats, pastas, some sort of shellfish thing that he'd never seen, and more. "I guess there are options."

"Looks like there's more to come," Kara said, nodding at tables covered in large metal boxes with steam escaping at the sides. "Maybe the secret way out is that you have to eat everything in here." She grinned up at him. "Want to skip the challenges and just try that? I bet I finish first!"

Owen began to blush. "Uh, I'm not sure we should—"

"I was *kidding*," Kara said, pushing her shoulder against his. "Come on, let's find something good."

This was all so *weird*. Owen watched her walk over to one of the tables and begin examining the options like she'd had breakfast here a thousand times. Who was this girl, anyway? Could she have actually met him before, a year ago? How could that be possible, even in the fictional world? He'd never been in her books before, after all.

A group of prisoners had already started eating, piling plates high with food, then seating themselves on plush cushions that looked perfect for napping. Next to the cushions were enormous TVs, what looked like some sort of virtual reality headsets, and holographic tables displaying all kinds of entertainment options.

All in all, the Jules Verne Memorial Time Prison actually looked really great. Five out of five stars, in terms of prison luxuries. If Nobody weren't about to ruin the entire nonfictional world, Owen could have seen sticking around for a day or two, just to enjoy himself. Maybe even a month. Not more than a year, for sure.

Farther away, a smaller group of prisoners had gathered near the exit, talking in hushed voices and pointing at the door. The Countess seemed to have noticed them, though, and was walking over, which didn't bode well. The group near the exit saw her approaching and quickly dispersed, all but one man who was concentrating on the door.

"Now, now, I wouldn't do that if I were you," the Countess said, loud enough for half of the room to hear her. Everyone turned, though when they saw who it was, many of the prisoners immediately found something else to pay attention to. Looked like a lot of the prisoners recognized the woman, even if Kara didn't.

The prisoner at the exit door turned around, and Owen

gasped. Half the man's face had been replaced by metal spikes, and he towered over the white-haired woman by at least two feet. But as soon as he saw the Countess, the man immediately dropped to his knees, his hands clasped in front of him like he was begging. "I wasn't going to touch it, I swear!" he said, his rough voice cracking. "We were just talking about the odds of guessing the right code. That's it!"

The Countess raised a glowing glove and slowly brought it close to his nonspikey cheek, stopping just an inch away as the man shook in terror. "*No one* touches this door," the Countess said quietly, yet somehow Owen heard her clearly. "Not until I have the code. Anyone who tries to activate it will find themselves . . . out of time." She made a fist with her glove, and it glowed even brighter. "Am I making myself clear?"

The prisoner with the metal face nodded over and over, as did many of the rest of the prisoners in the room, even the ones deliberately not watching.

The Countess smiled, then brought her glove to the man's cheek. He screamed, but the glove stopped glowing a second before touching him, and the Countess laughed. The man screamed again, then leaped to his feet and sprinted off down a hall as the woman turned to the other assembled prisoners. "Now, the way I see it is this," she said. "You can do what the guards want you to do, which is spend the rest of your pathetic lives here. Or you can each pick a door and bring me back the exit code. Anyone who helps me will be welcome to leave when I do. Anyone who doesn't is going nowhere. Anyone who tries to stop me, however . . ." She held up her glowing glove.

Someone coughed, breaking the silence, and several of the prisoners began to move toward the air locks, where groups began to form.

"Come on," Kara said, pulling Owen away. "Don't worry about her." She moved him to a table with food on it. "Seriously, eat something. You'll need energy for the rest of the day."

She grabbed a pancake, poured syrup on it, rolled it up, and began eating it as she waited on Owen. He just watched her, feeling sick. "How can you eat after that?" he asked her.

"Because pancakes," she said, finishing it, then licking the syrup off her fingers. She rubbed her fingers on Owen's arm and smiled when he pulled away with a yelp. "Seriously, we don't know what these challenges are going to be. You're going to get hungry."

"I'll be okay," he said, trying not to hear the spiked-faced prisoner's shrieks in his head.

Kara seemed doubtful, but nodded. "Then I guess it's time to get started." She pointed at the three air locks. "Ready?"

YES, LET'S DO THIS.

Turn to page 83. ◆❯

MAKE OWEN TRY THE EXIT CODE.

Turn to page 132. ◆❯

FORGET ALL OF THIS. MAKE OWEN SPEND THE WHOLE DAY JUST EATING AND PLAYING VIDEO GAMES!

Turn to page 326. ◆❯

AIR LOCK ONE.

The thought banged around in Owen's head so hard it echoed. That had to have been on purpose. He winced at the pain but kept his thoughts under control as best he could. *Don't blame the readers. This is* Nobody's *fault.*

Besides, if this was the only way to save Bethany, then he didn't really have any choice but to listen to them, did he? Assuming the readers hadn't decided *that* for him too.

"Might as well start with the first one," he told Kara, pointing at the fast-forwarding clock. They walked over to where a small group of prisoners already stood, each one waiting for someone else to open the air lock.

"You do it," said a tall, thin man to a woman with bulging muscles.

"So I get hit with this 'challenge' first?" the woman said with a sneer. "Not likely."

"Well, someone better open it," the thin man hissed. "Otherwise, the Countess might decide to come with us, and we'll probably all get turned into dust!"

Owen glanced back at the prisoners who'd chosen to stay behind and just enjoy the food and entertainment. When this was all over, hopefully those prisoners wouldn't turn out to be the smart ones. "See, I told you to eat," Kara said, bumping him again with her shoulder. "Look at you, you're practically drooling. Never miss breakfast, Owen. Most important meal of the day, I hear." With that, she grabbed his hand and pulled him through the group of prisoners to the air lock. "Ready?" she asked, then turned the large circular handle on the door without waiting for a response.

The air lock opened, and Kara led the group inside to what looked like every air lock Owen had ever seen in a science-fiction movie: basically a short room with large doors on either end, each one locked with a wheel. As soon as they were all inside, the door abruptly closed behind them, and red lights began flashing as a siren rang out in short bursts, like an alarm clock.

"Hey, no one said we'd be stuck in here!" one of the prisoners yelled, frantically trying to open the door they came through. And then the lights and siren stopped completely, and the air lock door on the opposite side opened.

A wave of humid air crashed over the group, bringing with it an assortment of odd odors—some typical jungle smells, others something like rotten meat. Owen swallowed hard, glad he hadn't eaten now. Rotten meat smell was *never* a good sign.

Loud, piercing noises buzzed by the open air lock door, almost too quick to hear. And the sunlight was so bright that Owen had to cover his eyes. When he could see again, he found himself looking at a pathway leading into the jungle. Was this a way out of the prison?

"Are they letting us outside?" Kara asked him, mirroring his thoughts. "Would they actually do that?" She paused. "Though I *have* always wanted to meet a dinosaur."

"You don't meet a dinosaur, girl," one of the prisoners nearby told her. "If anything, they turn *you* into meat. They're some of the most efficient predators that ever existed. Trust me, I've hunted a few."

Kara glared at him. "No wonder they threw you in here," she said. "Does that make you feel like a big man, to take down an animal by using futuristic guns?"

The prisoner rolled his eyes and moved toward the door, while Kara made rude gestures behind him. "I hope he gets eaten," she whispered to Owen. At his shocked look, she shrugged. "Okay, not *really*. Maybe just a little. Besides, he'll come back when the day is over . . . and then hopefully be eaten tomorrow, too."

In spite of himself, Owen shoved her with his shoulder, mimicking her move. "You're in a good mood now."

"Horrible people bring it out in me," Kara said as the group followed the dinosaur hunter.

The prisoner strode up to the open door and glanced outside. A loud, high-pitched blip sounded just outside the door, then again, too fast for them make out what it was.

"What *is* that?" Owen asked, not sure he wanted to know.

"It almost sounds like a fast-forwarded noise, huh?" Kara said, stepping up next to the dinosaur hunter and peering outside. "I have a feeling these challenges aren't going to be that easy."

The dinosaur hunter snorted. "Stay behind me, girl. I've got this."

Kara's eyes narrowed and she stepped back, gesturing him forward. "Oh, be my guest."

The man nodded, then slowly stepped out of the air lock, looking all around him, ready for anything.

He instantly disappeared.

Owen gasped and yanked Kara away from the door. What had just happened? One second he'd been standing there, and then, without even a word, the man was gone. Two more high-pitched blips sounded one after the other, and then silence.

"Whoa," Kara said, and pointed at the ground. Owen looked over her shoulder, then felt queasy. Where the dinosaur hunter had stood, there was now an enormous three-toed footprint, almost as big as a person.

One of the prisoners screamed and tried again to open the air lock door behind them, but didn't have any better luck than the first prisoner. The rest of the group pushed back against the far wall, trying to give whatever was outside as much distance as possible.

Kara, however, kept moving toward the open doorway, in spite of Owen trying to pull her back inside.

"I thought this might be the case," she said, glancing out of the air lock. "Remember how the clock inside was moving faster than normal? I think that was a hint. It looks like they sped up time, but just in this area. That's pretty impressive, honestly." She looked over at Owen. "Somehow they'd have to separate this section of the world from everything else in the time line, then artificially run it ahead quicker than the rest." She paused. "Unless this isn't actually outside. That'd be easier by a little, I suppose." She shrugged. "Either way, it makes for some pretty quick dinosaurs."

"He just got eaten," Owen hissed, pulling on her arm again.

"I know, I feel a *little* bad about that," Kara said, frowning at the footprint outside. "But he'll be back to his obnoxious self tomorrow morning. And maybe he won't be so quick to jump outside if he's not trying to intimidate a twelve-year-old girl next time."

"This is game over, man!" one of the prisoners shouted from the back. "What are we gonna do now, huh? *What are we gonna do?"*

"Listen up!" Kara shouted, turning back to the other prisoners. "This air lock appears to be a safe zone. So if you want to stay alive, *don't leave*. Time will reset at midnight, and tomorrow . . . well, don't try this challenge again."

"We won't remember what happened, though!" the scared prisoner shouted again. "We'll just keep ending up trapped in this air lock over and over until—"

Someone punched him, and the prisoner slid down the air lock wall to the floor, unconscious.

"There's no winning this challenge," another prisoner said. "You saw what happened. There's no outrunning that thing, whatever it was. They're superhumanly fast!"

Wait. Superhumanly? Owen's eyes lit up, and he began tapping on Kara's arm, trying to be subtle. She looked up at him, then grinned. "Fair enough," she said, turning back to the prisoners. "Me and my friend here are going to get the code, though. I'd suggest the rest of you just stay put."

"What?" one of the prisoners shouted. "You're only children!"

"Shh, let them go," another said. "That's Kara Dox. Hopefully the monsters will tear her apart and get so full, they'll leave us alone."

"And on *that* note," Kara said to Owen. "Ready to do your thing?"

His thing? How did she know about the fact that he could speed up his own personal time? He'd asked Charm to give him superpowers back in Jupiter City, hoping to run as fast as the Flash or other speedsters. But she came up with a way for him to move faster in time instead. But when did Kara find that out?

That could wait, though. There were bigger questions right now.

"I can speed myself up," Owen said, beginning to vibrate his legs to get it started. "But what about you?"

Kara looked confused. "Just hold my hand. You'll speed up my time too. You've done it a bunch of times."

He . . . had? Sometime in her past (and his future, maybe?) he'd somehow sped her up alongside him? That was new. When had he learned to do that? And what if he only found out because Kara told him about it, and then his future self shared it with past Kara? In that case, no one would have actually figured it out, and instead, the information would just be stuck in a closed loop, and—

His head began throbbing, so he dropped the whole line of thinking. "Worth a shot," he told Kara.

"Just make sure to hold on to my hand," she told him. "If you let go, my time will instantly fall back to normal speed. And out there would be a bad place for that to happen."

She slid her hand into his, and immediately he began to sweat. He wasn't sure if that was due to fear of the dinosaurs, using his time power, or just how close Kara was, but he really hoped it was the fear. *Had* to be fear.

His entire body was buzzing now, and the vibrations moved from his arm into Kara's hand and up to her elbow. She started to jump in place, clearly used to this, as the other prisoners began to slow down around them. Outside, instead of buzzing squeaks and short high-pitched blips, everything actually sounded like a real jungle now. The squeaks turned into the buzzing of insects, and the blips . . .

The blips became low, deep roars, just like the ones he'd heard outside his prison cell window. And they were very, very close.

"Ready to make some dinosaur friends?" Kara asked him.

"Not even a little bit!" Owen said, shaking his head violently.

She smiled and stepped outside, pulling him behind her.

As soon as she set foot on the dirt path beyond the air lock, the ground began to shake all around them. Owen looked up in terror as a Tyrannosaurus rex emerged from the large leafy trees just to the side of the air lock.

The giant Tyrannosaurs rex roared, huge drops of saliva splashing Owen in the face as the creature bent down to devour him in one bite. "No!" Owen shouted.

THE DINOSAUR EATS OWEN.

Turn to page 6. ⬍>

THE DINOSAUR MISSES, AND OWEN ESCAPES.

Turn to page 117. ⬍>

omersville in the year 2054," Kara said, grabbing Owen's hand and hitting the bracelet.

They instantly jumped forward in time, and landed in what looked to be a very similar time to the present.

The year 2054 wasn't too far in the future, sure, but Owen was disappointed by how normal everything still looked. People's cars seemed to be driving themselves, but that wasn't anything new, and other than people chatting without any visible phone or earpiece, everything looked pretty much the same. A street sign saying HOUGH STREET was lit up in a fun electronic font, but that wasn't a huge technological breakthrough or anything.

More important than fun future changes, though, was that there was no sign of the Countess or her daughter.

"It doesn't look like we're being captured, huh?" Owen asked. *Don't flip back just yet, readers. This might be the place!*

Kara glanced at her bracelet and gasped. "I don't know how you did this, but . . . this might have actually worked, Owen! This place does seem to be out of sync with the Countess's time line." She shook her head. "I can't believe I just guessed the right moment randomly. It's not even remotely possible!"

"See?" Owen said, unable to hide his grin. "Sometimes it's okay to let the universe be in control, I guess. I'm pretty sure it owed you one. Or a few hundred." Inside, he couldn't help but whoop with joy. *Readers, you did it! Thank you! That was so amazing!*

For the first time since Nobody had caught him back in the comic pages, Owen felt surprisingly optimistic. "So!" he said. "How do you think we find this founder person?"

Kara furrowed her brow. "This is the right time and place, but the founder could be anyone. There's a reason the TSA kept it secret, so something like this couldn't happen. I still would love to know how the Countess learned his or her identity."

Ah. Right. Owen's shoulders deflated, and he decided that he must have just set a record for the shortest optimistic feeling in history. "Okay, fair enough. When was time travel invented, anyway?"

"When I'm twenty-five," Kara said. "So a few years in the past from here. Why?"

"Just wondering if it'd been around by now long enough to start up an entire agency to police it," Owen said.

"Don't forget, we're talking about time travel. The founder could have started working on it this year, then jumped back to the year 10,000 BC and finished it there. Anything's possible."

"So not only don't we know what they look like, but there's a possibility that they might not even have arrived yet?"

Kara shrugged. "No, they must be here, or the time line would have changed to be under the Countess's control. Still, you'd think she'd be here already. If she's not, maybe I'm wrong about—"

The Countess and her daughter blinked into existence across the street from them, and Kara yanked Owen to the ground, hiding behind some café chairs.

"Okay, I'm not wrong," she said, narrowing her eyes. "Seriously, how did I ever pick this time and place? What are the odds?"

Thank you again, *readers!* "Let's not worry about the odds," Owen said, glancing over the table carefully, trying to stay hidden as he watched the Countess scream at her daughter, then walk into a nearby building. "They're going in. We need to follow them."

Kara, meanwhile, hadn't bothered to wait, and was already halfway across the street, waving at him to hurry up. In spite of the dangerous situation, he grinned and ran after her.

The building the Countess had entered didn't look very special. Mostly, it looked like a generic office building where a dentist might work next to an insurance company. Boring, but it got the job done.

Inside, the Countess and her glowing glove were halfway up a large set of stairs with her daughter behind her looking annoyed. Kara had hidden herself just inside the doors, waiting for the two women to move out of sight. She put her finger to her lips, then slowly followed them up the stairs, with Owen one step behind.

At the top Kara peeked around the corner, then held up a hand for Owen to pause. "They're stopping at a room just two doors down," she whispered. "She's using her glove to age the lock into rust. Okay, *they're in.* Come on, we have to take them by surprise!"

Owen quickly jumped up the last two stairs and followed, only to realize that they hadn't brought any weapons, while the Countess had her glove of death and Dolores could freeze time in their veins. Maybe they should have thought this through a bit more, come up with a smarter way to handle things?

But maybe it wasn't too late.

Readers? You can give me a hint about what to do here. Look ahead, and tell me if we should run in and surprise them or try to find some sort of weapon first.

"Hold on one second," he whispered to Kara, grabbing her arm. "I think I can help us out."

Something crashed in the room the Countess had gone into, and Kara shook her head. "No time!" She grabbed his hand and slammed the unlocked door open, smashing it against the wall.

Inside the room was a scene that Owen wouldn't have believed even a day before. Dolores held an unconscious elderly man in a lab coat against a wall, while her mother moved toward what looked like a robot strapped to a table. Weirdly, Owen recognized it as one of the prisoners from back in the Jules Verne Memorial Time Prison.

"What?" the Countess shouted, whirling around on them. "How did you find me here?"

"How did *you* figure out who the founder was?" Kara asked.

Dolores grinned, dropping her victim to the floor. "The TSA stuck him in the one place no one could touch him, the time prison. TIME-R's cell was next to mine, and for a robot, he liked to chat. Probably didn't think I could do anything about it, being locked in there with him."

"DO NOT HURT MY CREATOR," the robot TIME-R said. "HE IS A MAN OF PEACE AND HAS CON-STRUCTED ME TO SERVE MANKIND, SPREADING JUSTICE WHERE I CAN."

The Countess laughed, bringing her glove down close to the robot. "Oh, this will be just a pleasure."

"Stop!" Kara shouted, and went for the Countess.

A super-fast Dolores slammed her into a wall so hard she slid to the ground, not moving.

"No!" Owen shouted, and started speeding himself up, but a so-fast-it-was-invisible fist pounded him in the stomach and he collapsed to the ground in pain.

"Try to have some dignity, Dolores," the Countess said, sneering at her daughter. "They've provided us with a gift here by delivering themselves for punishment. The least we can do is grant them a swift, if painful, death."

"Sorry, Mother," Dolores said, and moved toward Kara, hands outstretched. "I'll just freeze her heart, then."

"Try not to make a mess when you do it, please," the Countess said as she moved her own glove toward TIME-R. "Really, you'd think you were raised by wolves."

Dolores paused, annoyance flashing through her eyes, then continued on her way.

Owen pushed to his feet unsteadily, throwing one hand out to the nearby wall for support, then shoved off. He had to stop Dolores somehow! The bald woman looked over her shoulder at him with a smug grin. "Wait your turn, boy," she said. "You'll get what's coming to you soon enough."

He couldn't let her freeze Kara's heart! But what could he do? Even with his time powers, there was no way he could move faster than she could. She had too many years of practice with them, knew the powers better than he did.

Kara's eyes fluttered open, and she weakly put up a hand to defend herself, but Dolores smacked it down.

He might have enough time to push Kara out of the way of Dolores's hand, but that'd leave his own chest open for freezing. What would that accomplish other than getting himself killed first? He'd just be sacrificing himself . . . for her . . .

Right. So in other words, he'd be fulfilling Kara's destiny. And maybe it was time to just let go of control and see what happened.

Readers, I need your help! he shouted in his mind, then silently ran through a plan, imagining it like a movie. *Can you make that happen? Please, I think it's our only chance!*

There was no time to wait to see, though. With one last burst of energy, Owen leaped forward and shoved Kara out of Dolores's reach, then fell to the floor where Kara had been. The bald woman gave him an irritated look, then shrugged. "You really couldn't wait? Fine. You go first, then."

And with that, she touched her hand to Owen's chest.

UM, WE DIDN'T ACTUALLY *SEE* OWEN'S PLAN. BUT WHATEVER, GIVE HIM THE POWER TO MAKE HIS PLAN WORK!

Turn to page 157. ⬍〉

NO, HE DESERVES THIS.

Turn to page 81. ⬍〉

*S*TAY AWAY FROM THE WINDOW, IT'S TOO DAN-
GEROUS. LISTEN TO THE VOICE.

Owen nodded, thinking how right that thought was.

"Though your sentence extends for eternity, we wish for
your last day to be comfortable," said the friendly voice over
the speakers. "So please feel free to explore the prison at your
leisure, and partake of all the comforts we have provided."

A last day that somehow extended through eternity? How
did that make any sense? Owen's hands began to sweat, and he
searched around his small cell for clues as to what might be the
cause of his "last day." Was it some kind of airborne virus? Poi-
soned food? Or maybe just the obvious: the gigantic human-
crunching monsters just outside his window.

"You'll find that you're not alone," the speaker continued.
"Time criminals from across all of history have been brought

here for punishment. Of course, the Jules Verne Memorial Time Prison is not intended for rehabilitation, so none of you will ever be paroled or released. We do encourage you to be social, however, as we imagine it will make the day pass a little faster."

Owen slowly peeked around the corner of his cell and caught sight of several other people in orange jumpsuits out in the hallway. Farther away, he thought he could make out other people talking, so not everyone cared about hearing the rules, apparently. He pulled back into his cell, not wanting to be seen just yet.

"You're free to do whatever you like here at the Jules Verne Memorial Time Prison," the voice said. "Use your time wisely, though, as when the clock strikes midnight, *time will jump backward by one day*."

Owen blinked. Time would do what? Jump backward? He must not have heard that right. It sounded as if the prison would make them relive the same day over and over!

"Don't worry, though. We aren't making you relive the same day over and over."

. . . Oh. Okay. *Phew.*

"In fact, you'll have no recollection of anything that happened on this day. All of time will reverse, not just your surroundings. That means as far as you're concerned, today is the very first day you're here, while in reality it could be your hundredth, thousandth, or even millionth chance to live this exact same day. You'll be doing so, after all, for eternity."

Owen's mouth dropped open, and he slowly slid down the wall to the floor. This couldn't be real. By "last day," she *really* meant their last day. So they'd live the same day over and over, with no memory of having done it? How was that even *possible*? What kind of horrible punishment was this?

Another even more terrifying thought hit Owen. What if this wasn't even his first day here? How long could he have been trapped? Had Nobody already found Bethany? Had he managed to separate the worlds, too? There'd be no way of knowing!

Okay, panicking wasn't helping. Owen forced himself to take deep breaths as spots began to pop in front of his eyes. It was going to be okay. It *had* to be. This was a book about time travel, clearly, and the main character must have been sent here, to the Jules Verne Memorial Time Prison. And if the main character of this book was trapped in the time prison, then he or she was going to get out, or else there wouldn't be much of a book. It had to just be a matter of time.

Which meant there had to be a way that Owen could escape too.

"As to the matter of escaping," the voice said, as if listening to his thoughts again, "we don't want you wasting your precious time trying to figure out the prison's time travel technology in order to turn it off. Still, we're quite aware that many of you won't stop until you find a way out. For those prisoners, we will tell you exactly how to leave this place and time, if you so desire. However, I'd recommend that you instead enjoy the indulgences the prison has to offer and spend the rest of eternity relaxed in complete luxury."

"Tell us how to leave!" someone shouted just outside Owen's door, making him jump. Several other people chimed in from either side of Owen's cell. None of them sounded particularly friendly, which wasn't too surprising given that they were in a prison. Owen pushed himself farther back against the wall, trying to stay out of sight.

"To leave the Jules Verne Memorial Time Prison, you must input a three-digit code into the exit door on the north side of the common area. Don't worry, the door is clearly marked. However, if you input the wrong code, the day shall immediately begin again for all inhabitants of the prison, so we recommend against guessing. Your fellow inmates might not appreciate it!" The voice laughed.

"Great, so there's no way to use trial and error," one of the voices outside his cell said.

"It's only a thousand or so codes," said another. "Maybe someone will get lucky."

"You'd have no idea if you were trying the same number every day," a third prisoner said.

"Don't worry, there *is* a way to learn the code," the voice continued. "For those of you who choose not to live out your day in comfort, we have created *three challenges*. Pass a challenge, and you'll learn one digit of the exit code. We do ask that if you wish to attempt the challenges, please leave those who don't to their relaxations. After all, there are no guards or wardens on premises, so kindness is appreciated."

What? *There aren't any guards?* So all of these criminals could just murder anyone they pleased? Owen frantically wiped his sweaty hands on his jumpsuit, all of his calmness evaporating again. Deep breaths, deep breaths.

What would happen if someone was killed, though? Would they just reappear again unharmed when the day reset? Seemed like that'd make the most sense, though it wasn't like he wanted to test it out or anything.

"Directly opposite from the exit door are three air locks, one for each challenge," the voice on the speakers said. "The first digit of the exit code is found in air lock one, the second in two, and the third in three."

"Come on," shouted the voice just outside Owen's cell, and he heard footsteps moving away from him. "We'll split into teams and each take an air lock."

"However," the voice continued, "keep in mind that each challenge is not only potentially life-threatening, but we make no guarantees that you can finish even one, let alone three, before midnight. So attempting the challenges might mean you spend eternity in great danger, when the alternative is a wide assortment of food, entertainment, and interesting company. We of course suggest you partake of the latter. And don't worry about eating too much . . . you'll wake up the next morning without having gained a pound!" The voice laughed again.

The footsteps in the hallway stopped. "How do you know we haven't tried this before?" asked one of the prisoners. "We might have tried the air locks over and over and failed every time. We'd never know!"

"But if we don't try, then we're stuck here for the rest of our lives. Longer, because we'll never age!"

"Is that so bad? Get a load of that food out there. There are worse ways to live."

It seemed like most of the prisoners had passed his cell now, so Owen edged himself to the door, ready to poke his head around the corner.

He'd have to approach this very carefully. First thing he had to do was find the main character of whatever book this was and get close to them. That way, when they escaped, he'd get out too. After that . . . well, he'd be stuck in prehistoric times, but maybe the main character had a time machine or something.

Either way, he couldn't just stay here in his cell. Whatever was happening with Bethany, he needed to find her quickly, and that meant getting out of this stupid time prison as fast as possible.

With that, Owen slowly pushed his head out of his cell door.

And found himself staring into a pair of deep blue eyes just inches from him.

The eyes widened in surprise, and a cute girl about his age with dyed-pink hair cut just above her shoulders took a step backward. Her look quickly shifted from shock to something odd, almost like a mix of relief, anger, and strangely, recognition.

But that was completely impossible. There was no way anyone in the prison knew who he was.

"Owen," the girl said, her face settling on irritation. "What are you *doing* here?"

. . . Okay, maybe not *completely* impossible.

NO ONE SHOULD KNOW WHO HE IS.

DENY EVERYTHING AND RUN, OWEN!

Turn to page 89. ⬦❯

HAVE OWEN ASK THE GIRL HOW SHE KNOWS HIM.

Turn to page 103. ⬦❯

That was . . . my home?" Owen asked, full of confusion but not wanting to anger the Magister. "It can't be, *really*. It's impossible. I can't explain how I know that, but—"

"I saw it from the start, child," the Magister told him. "You come from the future of our old world. Your magic has been removed, but you have a strong connection to the worlds we now create still. That was the confirmation that set us on this path." He sighed. "I deeply regret what we had to do, removing the Naturalists' magic, as well as that of everyone left behind. Unfortunately, they left us little choice, and now you and future populations will suffer. Perhaps at some point the worlds might join again."

"No, but seriously," Owen said, not really caring anymore about angering the old man. "That's *not* my world. It can't possibly be. We came backward in time from Kara's dimension. That was her world, not mine!"

They must have floated down through the new planet's atmosphere while Owen was distracted, and Adelaine landed their bubble softly in a pristine green meadow. Wildlife unafraid of people grazed peacefully nearby. The Magister glanced around, then began chanting as more magic-users landed on the planet. The grasslands around them slowly transformed as a small village built itself out of wood and stone from the ground and nearby forest, while in the distance, a castle began to assemble itself.

"Come closer, child," the Magister said to Owen as the new town grew. "We should converse in private."

Owen wanted to give some excuse, *any* excuse why he couldn't go off alone with the magician, but the Magister gestured with his hand, and Owen found himself floating toward the old man anyway.

"You believe you recognize me, don't you?" the Magister asked quietly, when Owen was close enough that no one could overhear.

Again, Owen wanted to say something, but had no idea what. *Yes, I met you in a fictional book series right before you trapped me in a void, and then left me behind using my friend's powers to jump out of books. You also had an insane idea to destroy an entire planet full of scientists, so yes, I recognize you. Also, I'm very, very terrified of you.*

As memories raced through his mind, it occurred to him how much the history of Quanterium and Magisteria in the Kiel Gnomenfoot books matched what had just happened between the Naturalists and the magicians of Atlantis. In fact, hadn't Kiel learned that Magisteria and Quanterium had once been one planet, but the magicians had fled to create their own world after being threatened by science? Did that mean . . . was this new planet they were standing on somehow Magisteria? Could he and Kara have ended up in the history of Quanterium, before the magicians left? But that didn't make sense, unless Kara was from there as well, and—

"Do not be afraid, Owen," the Magister said, then sighed. "I am not the man you knew, though I do see in the mists of time that he will be a descendant of mine. I'm truly sorry that his descent into evil will cause you such trouble." He took Owen by the shoulders and bent down to get closer. "However, *he* is not *me*. Look closer, child."

Owen looked everywhere but at the Magister until a quick snap of the man's fingers forced Owen to stare him in the face. And now that he was looking so closely, he did still see a resemblance, yes, but differences as well. This Magister had well-worn laugh lines in his cheeks and was staring at Owen with what looked like compassion.

Could this man really be the Magister's ancestor? And if so, what did *that* mean?

"I've also seen from your memories that this world I've chosen will someday embrace the very science we left behind," the man continued. "Millennia in the future, this world will someday become . . . Quanterium." He wrinkled his nose as he said it. "And from there, my descendant will follow my lead and create another world for his people. Perhaps my bloodline is cursed to repeat the same mistakes until someone shows us the error of our ways." He smiled slightly. "And I see that in this case, someone will. One of my descendant's pupils, this Kiel Gnomenfoot boy."

"Um, okay, but he had some help," Owen said, then realized his part of this wasn't exactly the important thing. "I mean, yes, Kiel (and Charm and maybe me) did kind of bring the worlds back together."

The Magister nodded. "I'm glad, as I have such high hopes for this reality. For you see, Owen, I have also seen in your memories . . . a girl of two worlds. A half-fictional girl, as you think of her." He seemed a bit put off by the word "fictional." "Granted, you should be aware that this reality is no more fictional than the one we just left, despite the fact you think of that one as the nonfictional world. Both exist equally now, and neither could exist without the other."

The Magister's words took a moment to sink in, but when they did, Owen almost choked. "That really *was* the non-fictional world?" he whispered. It couldn't be. There was no way! Magicians had never lived on Earth, and those war machines were decades or centuries beyond any technology that had ever existed so far.

The Magister nodded. "That was your world, yes, but millennia in the past. I see that in your time, the Naturalists will have forgotten much of their technology, and are in the process of rediscovering it." He half smiled. "I also see that many doubt science's power. While that brings me no small amount of perhaps petty pleasure, it's the wrong path. The ideal would always be for their science and our magic to become one and coexist harmoniously, as they did in my youth." He winked. "Even if that was a very, very long time ago."

"So . . . you just created the fictional world?" Owen asked, his head aching from trying to wrap his brain around the idea.

"I mean, I know it's *real*. But this is where we get all of our stories in the nonfictional world?"

The Magister covered his eyes wearily. "I apologize for that. To create this reality, we did have to remove all magic from the remaining humanity. However, we left you connected to that magic, a window within your mind to the power you once controlled. From that connection, you can witness the infinite possibilities that occur here naturally, though you'll be unable to affect them." He paused, looking off into the distance. "At least, I assume you won't. And that the connection only works in that one direction. With magic such as this, there are very few definitive answers."

"You're talking about . . . our imaginations?" Owen said, rubbing his temples to stop the pain. "That's the connection? So when I'm daydreaming or just picturing something, you're saying that's me seeing into this world?"

"With your last connection to the magic that is your birthright, yes," the Magister said. "I realize this is a lot to take in at once—"

"Oh, *really*?"

"But I needed to help you understand so that you might bring your friend home. And I don't just mean the girl you arrived with."

Owen stared at him. "Bethany."

The Magister nodded. "If our realities are to have a hope of reuniting in the future, you must keep this Nobody person from separating them completely. I'm not clear how that connection might have created these portals you've seen, but your friend is a sign that the worlds might be ready to coexist again. You must find her, and together, you must stop Nobody before he completely separates the two realities for good. Neither can exist without the other, Owen. This reality would drift into unanchored infinite possibilities without yours to give us stability. And I would not wish to even consider what might happen to your people without your . . . imagination, as you called it."

Owen shook his head. "Trust me, neither do I. But I need to get to a different story . . . I mean, different planet. Or whatever. She's not in this planet's future . . . story. History. Whatever it is? Maybe?"

"You can call them stories," the Magister said, his eyes twinkling. "At the core, that's what we are, aren't we?"

Owen frowned. "I think at my core, I'm, like, seventy percent water."

The Magister smiled. "That you are, my boy. But just because you no longer have your innate control over magic doesn't mean it won't listen if you call. I will teach you a spell, something that you can use to travel between the different stories, as you call them, that we'll be building for ourselves. And you can use that to get yourself and Kara back where you belong, then find your half-fictional friend. Can I count on you to do this, Owen?" He gestured at the newly built city around them. "Otherwise, everything we've done today to save humanity's magic will be for nothing."

Owen nodded. "I'll do my best. Trust me, the last thing in the world I want is to live in the real world without any imagination."

The Magister patted him on the shoulder. "You will do fine. Now, I know you've used magic before. But this won't be the same as when you read from Kiel's spell book. I will imprint this magic within you so that you'll always have it." He concentrated, leaving his hand on Owen's shoulder, and began to chant.

A strange energy flowed through the hand into Owen's shoulder, then filled his entire body. His skin felt like it was on fire, and he gasped, but the feeling immediately disappeared, and the Magister removed his hand. "There," the man said. "Why not try it by opening a hole to a familiar story?"

Owen stepped away and waved his hand in the air, not sure what to expect. "I don't really know what I'm doing, honestly."

"The magic will take care of things for you. You just need to will the idea to happen."

Owen nodded and closed his eyes. He imagined ripping a page through reality right in midair, just as Nobody had done so many times, then put all of his will into that image. He opened his eyes, gritted his teeth, and raised his hand. *Readers, if you have a choice right now, pick the right one, okay?*

And with that, he grabbed the imaginary page and pulled.

A hole ripped open, revealing a pleasant forest glen with a little cottage in the middle of it. Here and there were signs of what had been a world-shaking fight between a fairy god-mother and a genie.

"Well done, child," the Magister told him. "This power should serve you well on your journey." He chanted some-thing else, and an item appeared in the Magister's hand out of nowhere. He handed it to Owen, who looked down to find Kara's time bracelet, now completely whole. "Oh, that might help as well. But go now, as Bethany must surely need you."

Owen couldn't help but grin. "You know, you're *so* much nicer than your grandson or whatever will be. You have no idea."

The Magister nodded. "We all have the potential for great good or evil within us, Owen. It saddens me that he chose the wrong path, but I understand. From the Naturalists' perspective, I committed a great injustice today, in spite of their attack. They sought imbalance, and I provided it. May you and your friend bring that balance back."

Kara walked slowly over to them, her eyes on the tear in reality. She pushed a hand through, and then her head. "How exactly are you doing this?" Kara asked, smiling up at Owen. "It's so cool!"

And now Owen finally got to say something he'd waited his whole life to say. "Oh, you know. Magic."

Turn to page 67. ⬍❭

We need to find out how this happened, *now*," Kara said, her eyes wild. She grabbed Owen's hand and started to program her time bracelet, then stopped. "No, she'll be waiting for us in our time. We need information first."

"We're not going to find out much at Mount Rushmore," Owen pointed out. "We need to get to a city or something. Maybe one's built nearby here in the future?"

"Oh, I can move us around geographically with the time bracelet too," Kara said, shaking her head a little too hard. "Sorry, I keep forgetting that you don't know yet how these work. When we first met, you knew everything about it. That makes sense, since I'm telling you now."

Owen changed the subject, unwilling to again get into how they'd met. "Um, but back to how we travel around—"

"Right," Kara said, shifting from foot to foot anxiously.

"Think about it like this. If we just jumped forward in time, like, five minutes, the Earth would have moved in its orbit around the sun, so we'd pop back into a different spot on the planet, or inside of the core . . . maybe even in the middle of space. So the time bracelets automatically compensate for that and move us to the exact same spot we left from." She fiddled with the bracelet, still holding Owen's hand. "That means they can also do things like . . . this." She pushed a button and the scenery around them disappeared, replaced by a very familiar-looking town complete with regular nonflying cars and people on cell phones. They might be a few years past the present, but not much had changed technologically yet.

For some reason, the very normalcy of it all made Owen feel a bit safer, even if he couldn't quite place where he was. He turned, trying to get his bearings, then almost choked as he found a thirty-foot-tall statue of the Countess standing with one arm outstretched behind him.

"Where'd you bring us?" Owen whispered to her as people passed by them . . . and through them. Apparently they hadn't stopped moving in time yet.

"To your hometown," Kara said, glancing around as if waiting for something. The last person on the sidewalk turned the corner, and she hit a button. "There. I kept us just out of sync until I was sure no one would see us appear." She looked down at his hand in hers, then smiled at him. "You can probably let go now."

"Oh, right!" he said, yanking his hand away. "Sorry! I, uh . . . so this is home?" If it was, nothing looked quite the same. The layout of the streets was familiar, but not the stores or buildings. Was this his fictional hometown? Or was this the version of his fictional hometown in Kara's story, but not, say, Fowen's? There was at least one way to know for sure. "I know where we can go to find out what happened: my mom's library."

This would answer the question of whose town it was. If the library still stood, then this wasn't the version that Fowen had burned down. And if it was gone . . . well, they could figure things out from there.

Owen led Kara through the streets, wondering what time and day it was, and whether he'd get in trouble for not being in school. Did the Countess's future even *have* schools? Wait, this was the future anyway . . . he might have aged out of school by now! Silver linings.

The thought occurred to him that he was wasting time here,

that whatever was happening in Kara's story wasn't really his concern. Bethany needed him, and if Nobody separated the fictional and nonfictional worlds, anything could happen!

And yet, the Countess escaping had been his fault. The least he could do was figure out where she was, so that Kara could take care of things like she was meant to. And then hopefully she'd drop him back in time a few days in the past. Maybe he could even warn himself about Nobody and make all of this never have happened in the first place?

The more they walked, the more Owen felt out of place. Some stores were completely gone, like Max's Scoops, where Bethany's mom used to take them, and Owen would get his favorite, a hot fudge sundae with bubble gum ice cream. Bethany and her mom both thought it sounded gross, but they were clearly wrong. But now in its place was something called a Disciplinary Center, and people sped up as they walked by, making sure not to look at it too closely.

Even more upsetting, the building that had been the police station was now some kind of temple to the Countess, where men and women in long gray robes entered and exited, carefully watching the passersby.

"It's just up ahead," Owen told Kara, rounding a corner.

He stopped in his tracks as two robed men almost bumped into them.

"What have we here?" one of the men said, raising a gloved hand that began glowing. "Children belong in school. Truancy would be against the Countess's laws, wouldn't it, brother?"

"It would indeed, brother," said the other, his glove glowing as well. "If they skip school, then how will they learn to love and worship the Countess as she deserves?"

"Indeed, brother," the first one said. He gestured for Owen to step forward. "Come, child. You will be punished in the Disciplinary Center, and then, whatever's left of you will be brought back to your school for further education."

Kara pushed in front of Owen. "You stay away from him!" She put up her hands like she was going to fight them both somehow, but there was no way she could handle two grown adults.

And yet both men took a step back in fear. "It's her!" one said.

"The devil girl from the sacred law texts!" the other said. "We must alert the temple!"

The first one raised his nongloved hand to his face and started yelling into it. "The evil one is here in the city, just as the Countess prophesied!"

"Kara, we need to jump out of here," Owen said, but she just turned around and patted his cheek with a small smile. Then she hit the bracelet and disappeared.

The second robed man gasped and leaped forward to the spot where Kara had just stood, looking all around. "Where did the demon girl go?"

Kara reappeared right behind him and kicked out hard, slamming the man in the backs of his knees. He collapsed to the ground and she hit the bracelet again, disappearing as the first guard leaped at her. This time she appeared above him and kicked out as she fell, hitting him right in the face. He landed hard on his friend, with Kara winking out before she touched the ground.

Finally, she appeared right where she'd started and grabbed Owen's hand. "C'mon," she said, and pulled him away. "We won't have long before more of these guys show up. Let's get to the library."

"What did . . . huh?" Owen said, looking back at the unconscious men as she led him down the street.

"Something my older self taught me," Kara said. She looked around carefully for any more of the Countess's guards. "Fighting's a whole lot easier when you can manipulate time. You could have taken them with your speed powers too, but I know that tires you out, so I figured I'd handle this."

"Yeah, that's . . . it does tire me out," Owen said lamely, barely following what she'd just said. "So, um, thanks."

She grinned at him, then turned forward, only to stop so abruptly that Owen bumped into her. "Uh-oh," she said.

"No more uh-ohs," Owen said, and looked past her to see what the problem was now.

They'd reached his mom's library. Except not only *wasn't* there a library, but there wasn't even a burned-out husk of one. Instead, another statue of the Countess stood triumphantly on top of a pile of burning books.

"This one's a personal message," Kara said, her voice low. She clenched her fists and gave Owen a long look. "You know what? I'm *done* with this. I don't care how it happened, or where she first showed up. I'm going to take her down, *hard*."

"No you won't," said a voice, and someone stepped out from behind the statue of the burning books. "Because she knows you're coming. Trust me. I've been there."

It was a man, but that was as much as Owen could tell from this distance, especially since the man had a hoodie covering his face. Kara raised her fists again, ready for another time fight, but the man put up his hands in surrender.

"Don't worry, I'm on your side," he said, and walked slowly toward them. "In fact, I think you both know me pretty well by now."

"Who are you?" Kara asked, not putting her fists down. "And what do you want?"

The man pulled off his hood, revealing someone in his early twenties with brown hair and a goofy smile. "I'm Owen Conners," Owen's older self said. "And I want you to come with me. You know, if you want to live."

Turn to page 25. ⬍❯

W ho's Fowen?" Kara asked, staring at the duplicate Owen on the monitor.

"My evil twin," Owen said. "Computer, when did this happen?"

"I am, of course, nothing more than a large timepiece, and have no trouble telling you that this occurred four hours, thirteen minutes, and twenty-eight seconds ago. Would you like the milliseconds as well?"

"No, that should be fine!" Owen said, glancing at Kara, who was already plugging the time into her bracelet. She grabbed his hand and moved to push the button to jump them back, but he shook his head. "Not in here. We're not going to try to stop him. I want to see where he takes it, instead."

Four hours and thirteen minutes in the past, they waited outside the observatory for Fowen to come out. Kara had them moving forward in time at 1.01 seconds faster than normal time, so they'd be invisible to Owen's duplicate.

Fowen emerged from the observatory, walked right through them, then made his way silently through the construction workers. He wasn't wearing a hard hat, but for some reason none of the workers even seemed to notice him, almost as if he was invisible.

That didn't bode well.

They followed Fowen down Jupiter Hill and into the city. Being slightly out of normal time definitely made handling the crowded streets easier, though again, no one seemed to be paying any attention to Fowen, while still giving him a wide berth on the sidewalk.

Moving quickly, Owen's double led them away from the downtown area and closer to what looked like a warehouse district. Owen had seen this area before, from the top of Apathetic Industries, and up close it wasn't much more welcoming. An enormous joke factory with a giant whoopee cushion on its sign sat across from Apex Chemicals ("Remaking the world . . . periodically!"). Beyond that were a few factories that Owen couldn't believe would exist anywhere but a comic book world.

"Ice Town?" Kara asked, pointing at one. "Is that an entire factory just for making ice?"

"Don't question it," Owen told her. "I imagine it's just a front for cold-powered villains. I bet you it's got an ice-skating rink in there."

Fowen avoided these and instead crossed toward a building at the end of the street, this one with an enormous jack-in-the-box at the top. Tip-Top Toys looked like it hadn't actually made anything in decades, as the entire place was boarded up, but somehow the clown hanging out of the jack-in-the-box looked nice and new (and exceptionally creepy).

Fowen walked right in the front door, which was unlocked. Owen followed, after shuddering at the clown staring down at them from above, with Kara right behind him.

After passing through a lobby, they entered into the factory itself, where assembly lines had stopped in midproduction of various teddy bears and dolls. Most were missing parts, heads and eyes especially, which definitely added to the general horror vibe.

Fowen moved to another large doorway, this one with a light glowing beneath it. He opened it and stepped inside, then closed the door behind him. Taking a deep breath, Owen released his hand from Kara's, and dropped back into normal time, while she stayed hidden as backup. Hopefully they wouldn't need it.

Owen slowly pushed the door open, peeking inside. A large vat of molten plastic (or so the sign on it said) boiled in the middle of the room as the fires beneath it gave off an eerie light. Fowen stood to the right of the vat, fiddling with the machine he'd stolen from Doc Twilight. He seemed to be alone, so Owen carefully shut the door behind him and crept toward his fictional self.

"Oh, *stop it*," Fowen said without looking up. "You really think we didn't know you were coming?"

Owen stopped in midstep, mumbling some not-very-nice things about his twin under his breath. "How could you have known?!"

Now Fowen *did* look up, and he seemed a bit surprised. "Nowen?" he said. "You're early. We didn't expect you for a while yet."

Um, what? "But you just said—"

"I believe he was talking about me," said a deep, gruff voice from the ceiling. A twilight-launcher rang out, and Doc Twilight came swinging down from the shadows. He landed lightly, and his cape settled around him so that when he stood up, all you could see were his white lens-covered eyes. "And given that there are two of you, I'm guessing you work with the Terrible Twos?"

"Not quite," said a new voice, and an old man with a long beard appeared out of nowhere, as if by magic. He gestured at Doc Twilight, and nearby chains snaked themselves around the superhero, then carried his struggling body up and over the vat of molten plastic.

The old man turned to Owen, and in the fire's light, he could just barely make out the man's face. "Hello, boy," the Magister said to him. "It's been a while, hasn't it?"

"No," Owen whispered, and slowly backed up, only to run into something uncomfortably squishy. Whatever it was wrapped around him from all sides, then picked him up and turned him around.

"Ah, Owen," Nobody said. "Your fictional self was wrong. You're actually right on schedule."

Turn to page 241. ⬥>

NOBODY IS RIGHT, OWEN. THE WORLDS NEED TO SPLIT.

This time, the thought didn't hit his head very hard, but it still almost knocked him over. "No," Owen whispered, shaking his head. "You can't do this to her."

"The readers have spoken," Nobody told him, nodding his head. He placed a hand on each side of Bethany's face, then paused. "Apologies if this hurts," he told her.

"No!" Doc Twilight screamed again, but it was too late. Nobody tore his hands apart, and Bethany split with a sound like a book being torn in half. Two Bethanys fell to the ground, each one looking like a whole person but somehow . . . not. Each seemed a bit dimmer than before, if nothing else, as if neither one was fully there.

"Bethany!" Owen screamed, and tried to push forward, but Fowen yanked his chains backward, pulling Owen to the ground.

"And now, the last portal," Nobody said, opening another page in reality. Behind it lay a night sky, with stars shining over a pirate ship and a beautiful-looking island. Nobody pointed at one of the stars, then moved his finger to the next star to the left. "There we go, the second star from the right," he said, then picked up one of the Bethanys. "And home you go!"

And with that, the featureless man tossed Bethany up through the page, into the night sky above the island, and straight at the star.

"You'll kill her!" Owen shouted.

"Actually, I'm returning her to the nonfictional world," Nobody said. "The portal from Neverland to the nonfictional world is the last one remaining open." On the other side of the page, Bethany sailed toward the star only to abruptly disappear. "And there she goes." He reached an impossibly long hand through the open page, then spread that hand out to cover the entire night sky. He grunted, looking like he was lifting something incredibly heavy . . . and then ripped something.

"And the final portal is closed," he said, sighing as he pulled his arm back in and closed the page to Neverland. "The worlds are now separated completely."

Owen couldn't speak. There was nothing to say. Above him Doc Twilight moaned, and Owen could hear the sizzle of tears hitting the molten plastic.

"And now, Owen," Nobody said, "I have a special life planned for you. You've become so involved with Kara Dox's destiny that I'm loath to separate you. So as a special gift to you, who have been through so much, I allow you to stay here in the fictional world. Enjoy your new life in her story, Owen. And hopefully now that the nonfictionals are no longer in control, your life won't be in danger."

The words struck Owen but made little impact. He couldn't even comprehend what had just happened. Not only had he failed at rescuing Bethany or stopping Nobody . . . but he couldn't get home, either? And Nobody was going to leave him in a story where no matter what Kara did, Owen always died?

"Enjoy your new life," Nobody said, and ripped a page open in midair to what looked like a normal city street. He picked Owen up and pushed him violently through the doorway. "Oh, and watch out for that car."

Owen stumbled into the middle of a busy intersection as cars came rushing toward him. He screamed, raising his hands to protect himself, only nothing hit him. He slowly lowered his arms, his heart beating like mad, and looked around.

"You almost got killed!" Kara said, staring down at him. "What were you doing in the middle of the street?"

"Kara?" Owen said, looking around. Somehow, he was lying on the ground now, just feet away from the intersection, and Kara Dox stood above him. "Did you . . . save me?"

Kara gave him an odd look. "Do I know you?"

Owen's eyes widened. Had Nobody inserted him into the story at the point that Kara first met him? What did that—

Dear Readers,

I hope this reaches you. I've spent the last decade and a half trying to figure out a way to communicate directly with you. It wasn't easy, and I know you didn't listen to me the last time, but I need to tell you something.

The fictional world is dying. You won't see it now, but in my time, in your future, the signs are everywhere. The infinite potential has become this reality's undoing, and there's no fixing it. The only way to save the fictional world is to change your mind. *Please*. Go back and fix things. Tell Nobody not to separate the worlds. Not just for me, but for all of you as well. Otherwise, all signs point to this reality being completely wiped from existence in the next few months.

This is the doom that Kara blamed herself for, but it's not her fault, it's mine. It's Nobody's. It's all of ours. To get you this message, I've had to put all of my life energy into this letter, trying to get it to the proper place and time, so that you still have a chance to change your minds. It's a sacrifice, but one I'd make for the world (and Kara) a thousand times over, if only you listen and believe me.

Please. If not for the fictional world, do it for

yourselves. Go back and choose the other option. Choose to leave the worlds connected. Otherwise, we're all doomed.

Your friend,

Owen Conners (age 27)

—mean? Had he just been doomed to live out his life in Kara's story? It wasn't like he could ever get back to his own world, now that the worlds were separate. And there wasn't anything he could do about that, not anymore. He just couldn't beat Nobody. No one could, except . . .

Except the readers. If they were still reading now, maybe he had a chance? As long as the story didn't end here abruptly, he could still get them a message!

"You might not know me yet," Owen told Kara, feeling strangely optimistic. "But trust me, we're going to be good friends."

She frowned. "This is one of those time travel things, isn't it." She showed him the bracelet on her hand. "My older self just popped out of nowhere to give me this yesterday. So you're saying you met me in the future?"

Owen couldn't help but smile. "Um, not exactly. But don't

worry about that for now. First, we need to talk." He paused. "Are you hungry? I haven't eaten in days. Let's get some breakfast. It's the most important meal of the day, I hear."

Okay, now all he had to do was ask the readers to change their minds, and everything could still work out okay!

Readers, I . . .

THE END

And that's the end of the Story Thieves series.

. . . Unless you want to listen to Owen and decide to save Bethany. If so, turn to page 224.

The bald woman touched her hand to Owen's neck, and instantly everything went dark. He didn't even feel it as his head hit the jungle floor, and from there, Owen remembered nothing until midnight came and restarted the day.

Ah, readers. Knocking Owen out might be fun, I'll admit, but it's hard to keep the story going that way. Either start over at page 1, or turn to the next page for a second try.

A IR LOCK TWO.

The thought banged around in Owen's head so hard it echoed. That had to have been on purpose. He winced at the pain but kept his thoughts under control as best he could. *Don't blame the readers. This is* Nobody's *fault.*

Besides, if this was the only way to save Bethany, then he didn't really have any choice but to listen to them, did he? Assuming the readers hadn't decided *that* for him too.

"Let's do the second one," he told Kara, pointing at the stopped clock that only moved every minute or so. They walked over to where a small group of prisoners already stood, two of which were arguing loudly.

"You'll do what I say in there, or pay the price!" snarled an enormous man, the same one Owen had seen before, with the digital clock tattoos.

"That's not going to work for me, actually," a bald woman told him, her arms crossed, standing between the tattooed man and the air lock door. "So I might as well pay the price now, then."

The man snarled, then reached for her with both hands. So fast Owen could barely see her, the woman reached out with just two fingers and touched the man on the neck.

He instantly collapsed to the ground.

Every other prisoner in the group took a step back as the bald woman turned around. "Anyone else want time slowed down in the veins leading to their brains? If not, then stay out of my way."

She turned back and began turning the air lock's wheel to open it as the man on the ground breathed deeply, though still unconscious. What was with everyone in here?

Oh, right. They were time prisoners, so bad they had no chance of redemption. That was it.

Owen glanced back at the prisoners who'd chosen to stay behind and just enjoy the food and entertainment. When this was all over, hopefully those prisoners wouldn't turn out to be the smart ones.

"See, I told you to eat," Kara said, bumping him again with her shoulder. "Look at you, you're practically drooling.

Never miss breakfast, Owen. Most important meal of the day, I hear."

The bald woman opened the air lock, then moved inside. Kara grabbed Owen by the hand and led him in, the other prisoners pushing their way in too.

Inside looked like every air lock Owen had ever seen in a science-fiction movie: basically a short room with large doors on either end, each one locked with a wheel. As soon as they were all inside, the door abruptly closed behind them and red lights began flashing as a siren rang out in short bursts, like an alarm clock.

"We're locked in!" one of the prisoners yelled, trying to open the door they came through.

"Better in here than out there with the Countess," another murmured.

"What was that?" the bald woman asked, moving to stand next to the second prisoner. "Are you insulting the Countess?"

"Never!" the prisoner said, holding his hands up in surrender.

She stared at him for a moment, then shrugged and touched his neck. The prisoner collapsed immediately, and everyone else gave the bald woman a little more room.

Apparently even the Countess had fans.

At that moment the alarm and lights turned off, and the air lock door on the opposite side opened.

A wave of humid air crashed over the group, bringing with it an assortment of odd odors—some typical jungle smells, others something like rotten meat. Owen swallowed hard, glad he hadn't eaten. Rotten meat smell was *never* a good sign.

Weirdly, though, there were no sounds at all. At least not in the first few moments. As they all moved to the open door, though, a sudden onslaught of buzzing and roars hit them. But after just a few seconds silence returned, like someone had turned off a speaker system.

"What is going on out there?" Owen whispered to Kara.

"Can't be anything good," Kara said to him. "And why are they letting us outside? That doesn't seem right. Though I *have* always wanted to meet a dinosaur."

"Hope that you don't," the bald woman told her. "They're among the most dangerous creatures in all of time. Not counting myself, of course."

Kara rolled her eyes and started to respond, but Owen quickly shook his head and pulled her away. "I hope she gets eaten," she whispered to Owen. At his shocked look, she shrugged. "Okay, not *really*. Well, maybe a little. Besides, she'll come back when the day is over . . . and then hopefully be eaten tomorrow, too."

In spite of himself, Owen shoved her with his shoulder, mimicking her move. "You're in a good mood now."

"Horrible people bring it out in me," Kara said.

Abruptly sounds filled the air again, but just for a few seconds, the same as before. No one spoke until the silence returned, after which Owen noticed he wasn't the only one letting out a held breath.

The bald woman stepped up to the door and looked outside carefully. She turned back to the others and gestured for them to approach, which Owen and Kara did, along with one or two others. "You all should have noticed the stopped clock before we entered," the bald woman said. "This must be what it meant." She pointed out of the air lock.

Getting closer, Owen looked outside to see a dragonfly about the size of his fist, completely frozen in midflight.

"Whoa," one of the prisoners said, stepping out of the air lock. "They've stopped time? This will be easy to find the code, then. How dangerous can it be if time is frozen?" He laughed, then looked up and screamed. The man fell to the ground, still screaming, then scraped and crawled his way back inside the air lock as fast as he could.

The rest of the prisoners immediately pushed back against the entrance, one even trying to reopen the door again as the bald woman grabbed the screaming man. "What did you see?" she demanded.

"A monster!" the prisoner shouted. "It was going to eat me!"

"It sure was," Kara said, poking her head out of the air lock. "Owen, look at this."

Owen slowly peeked his head out of the air lock, then almost screamed himself. Standing above them with its mouth opened wide was a Tyrannosaurus rex, so close they could have smelled its breath . . . if it had been moving, that was.

"What if time restarts?" asked another prisoner, slowly making her way out of the air lock.

Kara stared at her for a moment, then grabbed Owen and the prisoner and yanked them both back into the air lock. A moment later, the sounds all kicked in and the Tyrannosaurus snapped its jaws closed right where they'd been standing.

And then the sounds disappeared, and the T. rex froze, his eye locked right on Owen.

"Smart girl," the bald woman told Kara, who was staring

at the T. rex head in fascination. "Time is frozen, but only for fifty-five seconds. I've been counting. And when it starts, it's only for five seconds each time."

Fifty-five seconds? That was all the time they had before dinosaurs had five seconds to hunt them down and eat them? That wasn't enough time to get *anywhere*, let alone to wherever the exit code might be.

But what choice did they have? It was either figure out how to use the fifty-five seconds they had, or stay in the air lock and be a free lunch when time restarted. Even if the dinosaur couldn't fit inside, they'd basically be stuck there until midnight.

Owen opened his mouth to ask Kara if she was ready, but the bald woman pushed him out of the way before he could say a word. "I'm getting all three exit codes tonight, before midnight," she said to the other prisoners as she quickly moved to the edge of the door. "Interfere or jeopardize that in any way, and I'll leave you to the dinosaurs. Now stand back, time's about to start again."

No one argued. Behind her the T. rex unfroze, and immediately it came right at the woman, but smacked up against some sort of invisible barrier to entry. Something seemed to be keeping the creature out. The T. rex pulled away just as time stopped again.

Without another word, the bald woman was gone, disappearing behind the T. rex. Apparently the barrier didn't apply to humans.

"Let's go!" Kara shouted, and led Owen out the door as well.

The feeling of walking right past an enormous dinosaur, even one frozen in time, made Owen's toes go cold. The creature's skin was like cracked leather and had various scars all over the place. As they passed by its feet, he couldn't help but stare at the three six-inch-long claws on each one and imagine what those could do to a human being.

"Forty-five more seconds," Kara declared, looking around. "We should probably get as far from here as we can and then hide."

Owen glanced at the T. rex's teeth and shuddered. "I'm with you there."

Together they set out at a run down the path, then pushed into the jungle as they ran out of time. When the full fifty-five seconds passed, the sounds of buzzing insects kicked in all around them. From the pathway they heard the T. rex roar again, and the ground began thumping, but it didn't seem to be moving quickly enough to reach them. Maybe it was confused about where they'd gone.

Time froze once more, and Kara nodded. "See? We've got such a head start that it's not going to catch up now. We'll be able to beat it to the exit code, no problem. This challenge is going to be so easy!"

"Will it?" asked a familiar voice behind them, and Owen whirled around to find the bald woman reaching a hand toward their necks.

THE BALD WOMAN KNOCKS KARA OUT.

Turn to page 126. ⬍〉

THE BALD WOMAN KNOCKS OWEN OUT.

Turn to page 316. ⬍〉

*F*ORGET ABOUT ESCAPE. YOU DESERVE TO TAKE IT EASY AND RELAX!

That's right, he *did* deserve that! After everything he'd gone through, between almost dying on Quanterium, his own fictional self trying to steal his life, getting stuck outside of the comic book world, and now being trapped in a time prison, wasn't it fair for Owen to take a short break? Was that too much to ask?

Owen turned to Kara, ready to make the argument that they should just have some fun for once, when he suddenly realized what he was about to do. What was he *thinking*? Bethany needed him! There was no time to sit around. He had to get out of here as soon as possible. And would the Countess let him sit around all day eating after almost killing him and Kara?

Ugh. Where had that thought come from, anyway? Was

he really that stressed out that his brain was rebelling? Something else played at the edge of his mind, something that he felt should have been obvious, but all the weirdness of the day wouldn't let him grab ahold of it. What—

"Are you okay?" Kara asked, putting a hand on his arm. He jumped at her touch without even thinking about it, and she pulled her hand away, looking hurt for a moment. Then she seemed to realize what she'd done. "Sorry. You must have been thinking about the Countess's glove. I didn't mean to scare you."

"No, don't worry, I'm just lost in thought," Owen said, feeling terrible without even knowing why. "And yes, I'm ready. Let's do this."

OKAY, *NOW* LET'S DO THIS.
Turn to page 83. ⬧〉

MAKE OWEN TRY THE EXIT CODE.
Turn to page 132. ⬧〉

Dolores slowly picked herself up as Owen's older self helped him to his feet. "Get to Kara," his future self whispered. "You can't use her time bracelet here, so open a page to a different story, travel back to the right time, then come back."

Owen was so tired, he could barely think, but he knew there was a big problem with that plan. "I . . . I haven't been able to open—"

His older self grinned. "Hey, it's me. I know. But guess what? I've got faith in you. You can *do* this, Owen. Trust me. I know you better than anyone."

And with that, he disappeared.

At the end of the hall, so did Dolores.

As fast as he was still moving using Dolores's time energy, Owen couldn't even make them out, beyond the side effects of their fight. Every so often one of the rebels would be knocked aside, or the Countess's guards would suddenly all be tied up in their own robes, just wearing undershirts and underwear.

Owen pushed off the wall and stumbled the rest of the way to the door at the end of the hall. He reached for the doorknob just as a hand tightened around his throat. Before he could move, another hand yanked the first one away, and both disappeared again.

This was *not* fun, standing in the middle of a war zone between two super-fast people . . . even when one of them was him! That made it worse, actually, since he knew that anything Dolores did to fight back would be hurting himself in the future. But there wasn't anything he could do to help himself now. He'd have to grab Kara and get out of here.

Owen grabbed the knob, yanked the door open, leaped through, then slammed it shut again. As the door closed, he felt something bang against it, but only once. Owen quickly locked it, not very sure that it would help.

He turned around and almost screamed in surprise. Kara was pointing a finger right at him, a worried look on her face. "Don't *do* that!" he shouted at her, before realizing she was just as frozen in time as the guards and rebels outside and couldn't exactly hear him.

He moved to her side, thinking she had probably been warning Owen's older self about the noises in the hall. Even though he'd most likely sped himself up in an instant, even a few extra seconds of time explained why he'd almost shown up too late to save Owen, whose entire fight with Dolores hadn't even taken a couple of seconds total, in normal time.

Just like he'd done back at the time prison, Owen grabbed Kara's hand, bringing her up to speed. She jumped at the touch, then stared at him. "Owen? What happened to older Owen?" she asked. Her eyes went wide and she grabbed his arms. "Oh no, are you okay?!"

Her touch sent pain flickering through his skull, but he nodded. "It probably looks worse than it feels."

"It'd have to or you wouldn't be standing up!" A fire began to rage in Kara's eyes, and she turned to the door, her hands clenched into fists. "*Who did this*, Owen?"

"It's the Countess's daughter, and she's . . . she's faster than I am," he said. "We can't go out there. My older self is trying to fight her, but I couldn't even see them. I have no idea if he's winning or not. She came with a whole group of guards, and we need to get out of here."

Kara shook her head. "We *need* to jump back about five

minutes, and ambush *her*." She tapped her time bracelet, then frowned. "It's not working?"

"She's doing it somehow," Owen told her. "All the other time travelers out there are stuck too. My older self said I needed to open a door to another place, use the time bracelet there, then come back here. That way we'll get out of her trap."

Kara stared at him for a moment, then shook her head violently. "No. We can't just leave him . . . *you*. We can't leave your older self here." She growled in frustration and banged her fist against the wall. "You don't get it, Owen! This happens to you *every time*, and I can't stop it! I can change anyone else's past or future, but *not my own*. But this time I'm not running away. I'm going to make sure he can't sacrifice himself for me again. If one of us is going to die here, then I'm going to make sure it's not *you*!"

Owen's mouth dropped open and his entire body went cold. His older self . . . was going to die here? *He* was going to die here, in the future? "No, you don't know that," he whispered. "He can beat her, he's so fast—"

"I *do* know it," she hissed at him, pulling him toward the door. "What do you think I've been trying to stop all along? I won't let it happen, not again!"

For a moment Owen wondered if he should let her go. If she was right, and his older self . . . if he himself in the future was going to die here, shouldn't they rescue him? But what could they do against Dolores? Even when not beat up, he couldn't match her speed. "If we go, we can stop this from ever happening, Kara. We have to restart the TSA, like he was telling you before. They'll throw the Countess back in time prison, and we'll have saved him because he'll never be here in the first place! That's our only way to fix this."

Kara banged her fist against the door. "Let me *go*! I'm not letting this happen again. Not to you, *not again*!"

Owen sighed and released her hand. She froze in time instantly, and he dropped his head into his hands. There was no time to argue. Right now, they had one shot at leaving, and even that would require Owen doing something he'd failed at every time he'd tried it.

He took a deep breath, then pictured a world he hoped would be safe, ten or fifteen years in its future. *This reality was created by magic*, his older self had told him. *And magic is open to any possibility, if you ask it.*

Having visited once already, Owen pictured a certain little cottage in the middle of a forest glen, destroyed during a fight between a fairy godmother and a genie. By now it should be all clear there.

Please, he thought as hard as he could, putting his hand up into the air. *Please let this work. I don't know if there's really magic out there, or if that's just how older Owen explained it. Either way, I ask whoever or whatever's out there . . . do this for me. I'm not a magician, and I'm not Nobody. I just need a door. Please. That's all, just a door.*

His fingers came together and he slowly pulled down, imagining he heard the ripping noise of a page tearing through reality.

Except this time there actually *was* a ripping noise.

His eyes flew open, and Owen almost screamed with joy as he found himself staring at a rebuilt cottage and a peaceful forest glen just on the other side of a portal into another book entirely.

Not knowing how much time they had left, Owen didn't bother grabbing Kara's hand. Instead, he prepared himself, getting into a runner's stance, then launched himself right at her, grabbing her around the waist and using his momentum to send them both through the portal.

"No!" she screamed, landing on the grass of the meadow glen. "Do you know what you just did?!"

Owen rolled over and looked behind him. The page was resealing itself, leaving behind Dolores, the Countess's reality, and his older self.

"I really, really hope so," he said quietly. *I hope you're going to be okay, older Owen. I'll do my best to make sure that never happens to you. I promise.*

"We have to go back, right now," she said, fiddling with the bracelet.

He took her hand. "Kara, we can't beat her. We need to stop all of this before it ever happened. You know what we have to do."

She gritted her teeth, then let out a deep breath and finally nodded. "You don't know what it's like, Owen. How many times I've tried to stop this."

"I don't know, you're right," Owen said, trying not to think about what was happening to him a decade into his future time line. "Maybe it's time to tell me."

She nodded. "Maybe it is."

Turn to page 67. ⬍❯

Y**ou're first in line, my young lad," the former Rotten Banana and now apparently Top Banana told Owen, holding out his hand to take an autograph book. "Only twenty bucks, or forty if you want me to write your name, too. Can't get my hand too cramped up, not with the celebration about to begin!"

"And what exactly did *you* do that's worth celebrating?" Owen asked, glaring at the supervillain.

The man looked insulted. "How *dare* you, child. I'll have you know that I led the assault against the Dark myself! I personally saved Kid Twilight and his friends on several occasions. You would still be filled with doom and gloom if it weren't for this newly ripened hero!"

Owen stepped up onto the stage and got right up in the banana's face. "Last I saw," he whispered, "my friend Charm was shooting you over and over for making banana puns. Now you claim you helped defeat the Dark? When exactly did *that* happen?"

The banana's eyes widened and he took a step back. "You know that horrible girl? She would have smashed me into banana paste! Thankfully, her friends were less violent, or I wouldn't even be here today."

Owen glared at him. "Here and now, I'm thinking Charm had the right idea. Did you turn my friends over to the Dark? Did you leave them there to be taken over by shadows? Where *are* they?"

The banana took another step back, waving his hands back and forth. "I don't know, kid, honest! Last I saw, they ran into the observatory to fight the Dark, while the rest of us distracted his shadows. It must have worked, because the shadows all disappeared a little bit later. But the girls never came back out, and when we went inside to look for them, all we found was the regular old Jupiter Hill Observatory. If that actually *was* Doc Twilight's secret hideout, we couldn't find a way in."

The Jupiter Hill Observatory? Okay, that was a place to start, at least. "What are you even doing here?" Owen asked the banana. "The Lawful Legion would throw you in jail if they knew who you really are."

"Listen, kid," the Top Banana said, getting more annoyed. "I don't know who you think I am, but I stepped up against the Dark. I really did save your friends a couple of times. Ask the girl with the red hair. Protected her from Kid Twilight in this very building!" He pointed at the Lawful Legion head-quarters behind them. "And they'd never have gotten into the observatory if it wasn't for me. So why don't you make like a banana and slip away?" He straightened his suit and smiled at the crowd behind Owen. "I'm sure there's a long line of people waiting to thank me, and hopefully buy some autographs."

Owen shook his head in disgust, then jumped off the stage and walked toward the street without waiting for Kara. She caught up to him just past the edge of the park and grabbed his arm to stop him. "Did the man in the banana suit say some-thing you didn't like?" she asked, trying not to smile.

"It's not funny," Owen said, a bit too loudly. A friendly-looking man put a finger over his mouth as if to politely sug-gest Owen quiet down. Owen glared at the guy, who just grinned and waved, then continued on his way. "That guy's a supervillain, and he was with my friends when everything went down. He claims he doesn't know what happened to them." He dug his fingers into his palms, suddenly realizing exactly how Bethany had felt for so long, looking for her father. The idea that Owen had left them behind, especially at the worst possible moment . . . it just felt like a weight bearing down on him, never letting up.

Behind them the crowds started shouting in excitement, and Owen turned to find the Lawful Legion flying, running, and floating out of their headquarters toward the stage the banana was on. For a moment he stopped to watch, hoping the super-heroes would throw the supervillain in jail, or at least punch him or something.

But then Captain Sunshine landed next to the banana and *shook his hand*. Owen groaned in annoyance as the banana raised both their hands into the air in triumph, shouting some-thing about thirty bucks an autograph. "*Augh!* I can see why Charm hated him so much!"

"Charm?" Kara asked. "Who's that? I thought we were look-ing for Bethany."

Thinking about the half-robotic girl Charm while standing next to Kara somehow made Owen feel guilty. "Both, actually," Owen said. "Or really, three of them: Bethany, Charm, and a girl named Gwen. The banana claimed to have seen them last at the Jupiter Hill Observatory, wherever that is. He said it was supposed to be the secret headquarters for Doc Twilight, Bethany's father."

Kara paused. "Whoa. Is that how she can do all the things you've told me she can? Because her father is a superhero?"

Owen wrinkled his nose. "It's a bit more complicated than that, but in a way, yeah."

"So, sounds like we should check the observatory first, then," Kara said, taking his hand and pulling him away from the park.

Owen sighed. "That's great, except I have no idea where the observatory is."

"Oh, just about a mile in that direction!" a grinning woman said as her child dragged her toward the Lawful Legion event. "Can't miss it, it's on top of Jupiter Hill! Just look for the giant telescope."

"Thanks," Owen said, forcing a smile in return. After seeing the banana, this whole cheery thing was starting to get on his nerves. Not that he really wanted the city to be like it was under the Dark, when an old woman had basically tried to murder them. But these people could *try* not being quite so upbeat just for a second. His friends were in danger, after all.

"C'mon," Kara said, waving at the lady. "We'll see what we

can find at the observatory and go from there. Between the two of us, I'm sure we'll figure it out."

"We could always wait and ask Captain Sunshine about it," Owen said, staring daggers at the banana.

Suddenly, the entire city went dark, as if something blocked out the sun. Owen glanced up, and up, and up, finally craning his neck back to see all of a giant toad at least a thousand feet tall standing on its hind legs, towering over the Lawful Legion headquarters. "People of Jupiter City!" it croaked. "Your heroes have been a wart on my backside for *too long*. And now the time has come for vengeance!"

The crowd went silent for a moment, then began to cheer. Captain Sunshine grinned, then immediately took to the skies, the rest of the Lawful Legion right behind him.

Owen sighed. "Okay, *fine*," he said, and began walking toward the observatory. "Of course a giant toad would pick now of all times to start a fight."

"*So* inconsiderate," Kara agreed, and shoved him with her shoulder.

Turn to page 50. ⬍❯

We travel back as far as we can," Kara continued. "Right to the beginning. Even if the Countess can track us from here, there's no way that trail will hold up before the planet exists. We should be safe there while we figure out what to do."

Right to the *what*, now? "I hate to bring this up," Owen said, "but how exactly are we going to survive without a planet? Don't we need air or even a place to stand? Space isn't that great for survival, I've heard."

"As long as we're moving through time, we'll be fine," she said, fiddling with the symbols on the bracelet. "The device has protective qualities that keep us alive. Just make sure you don't let go, or you'll drop back into normal time." She winced. "And if that's in deep space . . . just hold tight, okay?"

"Good tip," Owen said, grabbing her hand. She smiled sadly, then hit a button on the bracelet, and the entire world jolted.

Plants grew downward into the ground. Dinosaurs tromped backward through the jungle, sometimes even walking right through the spot where they were standing. Owen was so shocked, he almost dropped Kara's hand, but she squeezed his tightly. Apparently time travel made you insubstantial? That was convenient for them.

For a moment Owen wondered if that was something the author of Kara's books had put into place, or whether *real* time travel actually made you ghostlike. That moment passed when he realized there wasn't any such thing as "real" time travel, so that was sort of a silly question.

"Now that we're a bit farther away, I'm going to speed us up," Kara said. She pushed a symbol on the bracelet, and the world began flying by much faster, with flashes of animals going by too quickly to see, and day and night mixing into each other.

"How did you learn to use that thing?" Owen asked her, watching with awe the various changes in the world around them. The dinosaurs began to disappear, leaving just enormous insects and plants.

"My older self showed me," she said, and Owen noticed she wasn't watching the show in front of them but was instead just staring off into space. "It's not that hard, actually. The TSA made them pretty user-friendly."

"Except they're not around to make them anymore," Owen pointed out. "And wait, if your older self showed you how to use it, then how did she learn it?"

"Because I grow up and show myself," Kara said. "I know it doesn't make sense, but try not to think about it too much. Remember, paradoxes don't affect me." She squeezed his hand again. "Just part of my charm."

He smiled at that, and realized that in spite of only knowing her for a few hours, that's not how it felt for some reason. It *was* almost like he'd known her for longer. Maybe not a year, like she claimed, but certainly for days at least.

That made sense, too, if they'd had to do all three challenges to get the exit code for the readers. Owen briefly wondered what he'd found out about Kara in that time. Had she shared what this terrible future thing she was going to do was?

Or anything about this whole "immune to paradoxes" thing, which still made no sense? Paradoxes weren't like the TSA agents, police that punished you for breaking a rule. They were impossibilities of logic, a broken series of events that shouldn't and couldn't actually happen in the way that they did. How could an impossibility *not* affect Kara?

Yet here they were, using a TSA time bracelet that shouldn't exist, that Kara's older self had taught her younger self to use, only so she could grow up and teach her younger self again. It was a circle in time with no beginning.

"You're thinking about it," Kara said. "I can hear your teeth grinding."

"Fair enough," he told her, trying to unclench his teeth but failing. The world around them was entirely devoid of animals now, and the land seemed to have shifted. Mountains that had existed in prehistoric times were now flat plains, and oceans had moved in where there had been jungle a few minutes before. Either they were moving even faster through time, or the planet was going through some massive changes.

Kara glanced at her bracelet. "We just passed the first form of life on Earth," she said, then turned her head up to the sky.

"And no UFOs to be seen. Guess that means the planet wasn't seeded by alien civilizations."

Owen's eyes widened. "Is that . . . something people were worried about?"

She grinned at him, and it seemed more genuine this time. "I love how gullible you are. It just brings me joy."

The rocky ground melted into magma in places, and large meteorites lifted off the planet to rocket into space. Soon the entire planet began to dissolve into huge chunks of rock, and Kara squeezed Owen's hand. "Almost there. Watch. This should be fun."

The Earth completely fell apart now as a backward explosion created several larger Earth-sized planets, which flew off in different directions. A large wave of cosmic energy erupted through them in reverse, and the bracelet on Kara's wrist glowed an odd color as it passed. Never had Owen been so thankful that a no-longer-existing TSA had added a protective element to the time bracelets, and that the bracelet still existed thanks to Kara's paradox immunity, however that worked.

Some of the newly formed, previously-part-of-Earth rocks

fell into orbit around the sun, while some headed off in a direction behind them. "That way's the big bang, I'd guess," she said, pointing in the direction some of the chunks of Earth had headed.

"*Really?*" Owen asked, suddenly realizing how amazing that would be. "Can we go see it?" Sure, it'd be the fictional big bang, but still!

"Too dangerous," Kara told him. "It's not just matter that exploded into existence. Time did too. And the closer we get to it, the more likely we'll be sucked back in like a black hole. I'd rather not be compressed down with the rest of the universe into an infinitely tiny space, if you don't mind."

He sighed. "I do mind a little, but okay. If that's the case, shouldn't we slow down?"

She nodded, fiddling with the bracelet. Then she said, ". . . Huh."

For some reason, that one word brought the world crashing back down around Owen. "'Huh'? Good huh, or bad huh?"

"Not a great one," Kara said, glancing up at him with concern. "I think something might be wrong with the bracelet. It's not letting us slow down."

Those weren't the words he wanted to hear. "That *does*

sound like something very, very wrong. You can fix it, though, right?"

She frowned, still pushing symbols. "Um, not exactly. My older selves never explained how to fix them. It's not like you need to know how to repair a TV to watch a show on it, you know?"

"Except this isn't TV, this is *time travel*!"

"I do appreciate that point, believe me," Kara said, pushing more buttons, then looking up. "Um, I think we're actually going faster now. This *might* be a problem."

All around them, stars began sliding backward in the same direction as the bits of Earth had gone, faster and faster. In the opposite direction, a line of black, starless nothing drew closer.

"Might be a problem?!" Owen shouted. "We're going to reach the beginning of everything, which you just said we wouldn't survive! How is that not a huge problem?"

Kara nodded. "You're right. Let's say *probably* will be a problem. I think it might have been that cosmic energy wave that passed by us. Could have been too much for the bracelet?"

Owen began to hyperventilate, his hand sweating in hers as she kept pushing buttons. Was he really going to die before anything ever existed? Why couldn't a dinosaur have eaten him instead?

Wait! Could the readers fix the time bracelet? Was that something they could just declare had happened? If so, would they? *Please*, he begged. *Fix this or we're going to become one with everything!*

UM, *HOW* WOULD WE FIX A TIME BRACELET? LET'S JUST GIVE UP AND START OVER BY GOING TO THE FUTURE INSTEAD.

Turn to page 206. ⬥❯

LET'S SEE WHAT HAPPENS WHEN KARA CAN'T FIX IT.

Turn to page 43. ⬥❯

S TAY AWAY FROM THAT GLOVE, IT'S PROBABLY DANGEROUS!

The words echoed in Owen's head, as if he was screaming them at himself. He grabbed Kara's shoulders and cautiously pulled her away from the woman and her glowing hand. "Do you know who she is?" he whispered, assuming she'd have to, considering the woman clearly recognized Kara.

"Nope," Kara said, her fists still held up, ready for a fight. "Do you?"

"Oh, you wouldn't know me *yet*," the strange woman said, her glowing gloved hand stretched out toward them as she stepped closer. "No, it won't be until your future that you'll disrupt plans that I've been working on for over a half century now. Then you'll turn me over to the TSA, who will send me *here*." She smiled, showing all of her teeth. "If I'd known they were locking me up with you, however, I'd have killed fewer agents on the way."

Whoa. She'd killed people? How dark *was* this Kara Dox series? "So what does the glove do?" Owen asked, not really wanting the answer.

The woman's smile widened. "It devours time from your body, ravaging your physical form until it's a husk of itself, desiccated and mummified, after which your remains will collapse into dust."

Huh. Well, he *had* asked. "I thought it might just be for fashion," Owen said, and out of nowhere Kara laughed. She immediately covered her mouth with her hand, but by then it was too late.

"You *dare* mock me?" the woman said, her eyes widening with crazed rage.

"Did you ever think that attacking me now might be what makes me come after you in the future?" Kara asked, thankfully changing the subject. "Maybe you're creating a self-fulfilling prophecy. It's not too late, though. If you leave us alone now, then I'll make sure to return the favor and not interfere with whatever your plans are." She paused. "Though maybe I should ask what those plans *are* before I promise."

"First, I made sure the TSA was never created," the woman said, slowly advancing toward them. "Then, with no one to stop me, I sent my past and future selves elaborate plans and specific periods they should travel to. Hundreds of versions of me installed themselves into positions of power throughout history." She curled her gloved hand into a fist. "I would have ruled everything, forever!"

Kara wrinkled her nose. "I'm not entirely sure that makes sense, but either way, that does sound like something I'd fight, just on principle." She glanced back at Owen and smiled shyly. "How about you?"

Owen stared at her in shock. "Um, I'm good with it!" He lowered his voice and talked faster. "Especiallyifit'sjustsomething-wetellherrightnowsosheleavesusalone!"

"Ah, young man, I'd never take you at your word," the woman said, smiling again. "If you honestly intended not to interfere, then I wouldn't have been thrown in this prison. But since I'm still here, you clearly can't be trusted."

"But if you weren't here, then we'd never be able to say we wouldn't interfere to begin with," Owen said, hoping his logic was correct. "Isn't that a paradox?"

"Paradoxes don't affect me," Kara whispered at him.

"Paradoxes don't affect her," the woman said at the same time.

Um, okay. "I feel like I've missed something," Owen whispered to Kara.

"I'll tell you later," Kara said, then turned back to the woman. "Okay, you're right, I would normally stop you. But I'm not leaving here, so whatever my future self did in your time line, she won't be doing it anymore. I gave myself up, and I'll be staying in this prison for the rest of my life."

The woman waved her glowing hand impatiently. "Again, if you did, *I wouldn't be here*. No, clearly my only chance is to kill you once and for all. It might create a paradox, but I'm willing to take that chance. At the very least, it'll be immensely satisfying. And if time starts over in the prison and I get to kill you day after day for the rest of eternity, it will be a small consolation for what you've stolen from me!"

Owen and Kara took another step backward, only this time Owen hit the wall at the end of the hall. They were out of room.

"I don't even know your name, you know," Kara said as the woman advanced.

The woman sneered. "Of *course* you don't. You think I'm going to let you find out my real identity, then wipe me from time altogether? No. You can call me the Countess." She stretched her glowing glove out toward them. "Now, please, *beg for your lives*. I would really like to enjoy this as much as I can."

Kara stepped forward, turned, and gave Owen a sad look. She sighed, then turned back to the Countess. "Leave him alone, and you can do whatever you want to me."

Whoa, what? She couldn't be serious. Was this just a bluff? He didn't even know this girl, and now she was sacrificing herself for him?

The Countess sighed. "It's not begging, but it will have to do." She brought her glove closer to Kara, who flinched but didn't move away.

"No!" Owen shouted, leaping forward. The Countess immediately aimed her glove at him, and he raised both hands in surrender. "You'd be making a huge mistake if you, um, olden her!"

"Would I now?" the Countess asked with a smug smile, her hand getting closer to him.

"Yes," Owen said, subtly pushing Kara backward again. "Because we're going to figure out how to get out of here, and that means we can get you out too."

The Countess's glove froze in midair, and she began to laugh.

"You have no idea how this prison works, do you?" she said. "The challenges will require a day to complete each, after which point time will start over, and you'll forget whatever part of the code you found. It's a system designed to keep you busy, you fool. There *is* no escape! Maybe with a week of regular time we could figure out how to shut down the twenty-four-hour reversal, but not if we have to start over every day."

All right, yes, good point. But if this was Kara's book, there had to be some way out of this. But how? If they really did forget every day, maybe there was some way of leaving a message, writing a note, something like that? If only they could call someone and report the exit door code digit after each challenge, or . . .

Wait a second. There *was* a way for someone to make a note about what the code was, even if all the prisoners forgot. This was a Pick the Plot book! That meant the readers themselves would see the code, and maybe they'd be able to input it into the book somehow!

Sure, Owen had no idea how that last part would work, but that had to be it. This was a challenge for both them *and* the readers. Which meant they actually *could* escape!

But how exactly could he explain that to the Countess?

"Let's just say that we have a way of keeping track of the code digits that we find," he said, sounding a lot less sure of himself now that he had to spell it out. "Outside of this, uh, time line."

"And how exactly will you accomplish this feat?" the Countess asked.

"Um?" Owen said brightly, looking at the ceiling.

Kara leaned over and whispered in his ear. "Is this one of those nonfictional things I hate hearing about?"

Owen's eyes widened, but he nodded quickly at her. She nodded back, looking uncomfortable with the whole subject, then turned to the Countess. "You know I'm immune to paradoxes. Well, I'm also immune to time distortions. I'll keep my memory through each day of this prison, which means I'll be able to remember the code."

The Countess sneered, raising her glove again. "If that were true, they'd never have locked you in here."

"They would if I turned myself in voluntarily," Kara told her.

This made the Countess pause, as if she was considering. "I *should* just kill you now and take my chances."

"You could, but we both know you're not sure if my immunity to paradoxes will leave you locked in here," Kara told her.

"If you were positive, you'd have already done it. So what'll it be?"

The Countess gritted her teeth, then lowered the glowing glove. "If you are lying, I will find out, and I *will* make you suffer. Then when I escape, I will wipe you from history, followed by your parents, and then all of your ancestors back to the dawn of mankind. *This* I swear to you now."

"Then it sounds like we've got a deal," Kara said, not sticking her hand out to shake.

YIKES. SOUNDS LIKE KARA AND OWEN SHOULD GO FIND THE CHALLENGES.

Turn to page 252. ⬧⟩

SNEAK ATTACK THE COUNTESS!

Turn to page 250. ⬧⟩

Okay, readers. We're not going to go into the grisly details, but suffice it to say that Owen will awaken the next morning in one piece. However, I did mention that this book was meant to teach Owen a lesson, not feed him to hungry carnivores. Please, for the sake of the fictionals around him, try to be less bloodthirsty. Now either start over on page 1 or instead jump forward a bit and have the dinosaur not eat Owen this time by turning to page 170.

DO WHAT THE ROBOT SAYS. HE'S A ROBOT, THEY'RE SMART!

Owen growled in frustration as his body moved almost against his will toward the gigantic T. rex and the robot he'd almost finished undevouring. "We're going to get eaten!" he hissed at Kara, who was in front of him.

"Look behind you, slowly," Kara said, and Owen turned his head, then gasped. Several velociraptors had run straight at them backward, then turned around and begun walking toward them slowly, their eyes up on the T. rex. "This all makes sense if you think of it in reverse!"

"No, it really doesn't," Owen whispered, backing away from the raptors, hands held up in surrender. But they didn't seem too concerned with him and were watching the T. rex warily instead.

"HUMANS, THE CREATURE IS REPLACING MY FOOT NOW, SO I WILL MOMENTARILY BE AVAILABLE FOR FLEEING BACK TOWARD THE AIR LOCK," TIME-R said, still on the ground. "YOU HAVE OF COURSE FIGURED OUT WHAT IS HAPPENING HERE?"

"No!" Owen shouted at him, while Kara nodded.

"Just follow me and I'll explain as we go," Kara told him, grabbing his hand and pulling him toward the robot. The T. rex had put one last foot back into place as TIME-R slowly stood up. "See, this all happened already. The T. rex probably chased the three of us here, then caught the robot. While it ate him, that gave us time to get to the top of the volcano." She turned around and nodded at the slowly advancing raptors. "And these guys probably were chasing us, then saw the T. rex and let him have us. But they must have stuck around to see if there'd be anything left, and only now decided to give up and turn to run away, since they figure they're not going to get any part of us or the robot."

Owen's brain pounded, and not from the readers yelling at him. "Okay, fine," he said as the T. rex began running away from them backward down the path. The raptors shortly followed, and the robot gestured for them to come too as it ran smoothly after the group. "But I want it on record that this is all clearly overcomplicated!"

"So recorded," Kara said with a half smile as they ran down the path.

Up ahead several trees covered in giant leaves had fallen in the middle of the path, and TIME-R pointed at them. "THOSE TREES WERE PUSHED OVER. YOU CAN SEE THAT BY THE MARKS ON THE BARK. I HYPOTHESIZE THAT—"

"We were up in the trees, and the T. rex knocked them over!" Kara shouted, and pulled Owen toward one of the trees as the T. rex slowed and backed away. The raptors did the same, giving them lots of space around the fallen trees. Owen shook his head as Kara left the sign on the ground, then lay down on the trunk, grabbing for handholds. This was all just madness. But what else could he do but follow her lead?

Owen lay down just above her as Kara continued. "See, now we just need to wait for—"

The T. rex roared and came running at them, only to stop a few feet away and shake itself as if in pain. Both TIME-R's tree and theirs rose magically into the air, theirs first pushing TIME-R's tree into place, then slamming into the dinosaur's head. The T. rex ran backward a few yards away as both of their trees planted themselves firmly into the ground.

"Cool, huh?" Kara said, grinning in spite of the danger.

"No!" Owen shouted. "And if you hadn't noticed, now we're stuck in a tree!"

On the ground now, raptors were appearing (backward) from the jungle, flowing out onto the path. Then more surprisingly, several shocked-looking prisoners poked their heads out from between the leaves. "You do *not* want to know what just happened to me!" one of them shouted.

"What is going on?" another said as the raptors began to run backward toward the air lock now, giving Owen, Kara, and TIME-R some room to climb back down. Once they hit the ground, Kara pulled Owen away, leaving TIME-R to explain the situation to the others.

"Don't tell them about the sign," she whispered, grabbing it as they moved down the path. "The last thing we need is for any of these other prisoners to escape. There's a reason they got locked in here."

"Hey, that girl's got something in her hands!" the prisoner with the eye patch shouted. "Get her!"

"Run!" Owen screamed, and grabbed Kara's hand, then sprinted off toward the retreating pack of velociraptors. A moment later the group of prisoners had moved to follow, and Owen really wished he had time to stop and just marvel at how odd this scene must be: two kids chasing a group of dinosaurs running backward while being chased by a group of prisoners forward.

All in all, this had to be the worst challenge. Had to be.

"There's the air lock!" Kara shouted, and sped up. The raptors began to split off into the jungle to the sides of the path, which was good, since Owen had no idea what would have happened if they'd actually caught up to the creatures. More prisoners popped up out of the woods, and Owen had to try really hard not to think of how many of them had been eaten during this challenge.

"As soon as we get into the air lock, we need to lock the door!" Kara shouted as they got closer. Owen nodded, not sure he had the breath to answer, but ready to do whatever he could to keep the time prisoners from torturing them for . . . well, whatever the sign was. TAKE ME wasn't exactly the clearest of instructions, but they hadn't had much else to go on.

They passed into the air lock, only to have another bright

light flash over them, strong enough to stop Owen in his tracks. "Kara?" he said, her hand slipping out of his.

"I'm here!" she said from his side as the light faded. "Also, uh-oh."

The light faded, and they found themselves surrounded by prisoners.

"DINOSAURS ARE THE MOST EFFICIENT KILLERS IN RECORDED TIME," TIME-R was saying. "I WOULD HAVE SUPPOSED THAT A HUMAN BEING MIGHT NOT WANT TO MEET SUCH A CREATURE, AS SHE WOULD SURELY BE EATEN BY IT."

Owen's eyes widened, and he glanced around at the rest of the group. None of the prisoners seemed particularly interested in him or Kara. In fact, they were all staring out at the path beyond the air lock.

"Well, let's see what's out there, then," the woman with the eye patch said. "And hopefully there won't be any dinosaurs."

The prisoners began to file out of the air lock, while Owen and Kara slipped to the back of the group, waiting for the rest to leave. Finally, when all had, Owen turned to her and gave her a look of terrified confusion. "Huh?!" he said.

"I guess this is the forward version of what we just did backward?" she said. "I'll tell you what, though . . . I say we just sit this one out. It might create a paradox, but stick by me and we'll be fine."

"I'm down for waiting in the air lock until midnight," Owen agreed, then noticed something. "Wait. How do you still have the sign if we haven't started yet?"

Kara looked down at it in surprise. "The writing's changed too." Instead of TAKE ME, the sign now just had a numeral "0" on it.

"That's the exit code," Owen whispered, and grinned at her. "The challenge must be set up to finish it in reverse, and it leaves you with the code! So . . . we did it?"

She smiled back, then hugged him. "Of course we did. What can't we do?"

Other than get out of the prison? Owen sighed, then turned his thoughts inward. *Did you get that, readers? The third number is zero. Three is zero. Three is zero. Got it?*

There wasn't a response, but right now, Owen's brain couldn't take a reader command anyway, so he happily slid down the air lock wall. Ignoring the screams outside, he and Kara waited out the rest of the day, until night finally came and reset the clock.

WELL, *THAT* WAS WEIRD. TURN BACK TO PAGE 1 . . . OR CHEAT A BIT, AND SKIP TO THE DECISIONS ON PAGE 259.

WAIT, THIS WAS WEIRD. TURN BACK
TO PAGE 1 . . . OR CREATE A QUEAND
SKIP TO THE DECISION BOX ON PAGE 136.

*P*UNCH YOURSELF IN THE FACE. HARD.

Owen's hand clenched into a fist, and before he knew what was going on, it swung for his face. He yelled in surprise and barely managed to get his other hand up to block it. He fought his fist back down to his side as Kara just stared at him.

Oh, so that's *how it's going to be? Two can play that game!*

And with that, he punched his rogue fist with his other hand as hard as he could.

Pain shot through both hands, and Owen doubled over, keeping silent but screaming in his mind.

"Something is very, *very* wrong here," Kara said.

"No, really, everything's fine," Owen told her from between clenched teeth. "I'm totally good. Now I'm going to choose which air lock to do first. Ready?"

She just gave him a confused look, and he took that as the closest to a yes he was going to get.

Real funny, readers. Great. You've proven you can mess with me. Now how about we get on with the choice? If not, we're all stuck here, including you. So unless you want to keep reading about nothing happening, maybe choose something that will move this story along!

HAVE OWEN PICK AIR LOCK ONE.

Turn to page 260. ⬍❯

HAVE OWEN PICK AIR LOCK TWO.

Turn to page 317. ⬍❯

HAVE OWEN PICK AIR LOCK THREE.

Turn to page 110. ⬍❯

Author photograph by Maarten de Boer

Strangely enough, JAMES RILEY, bestselling author of the Half Upon a Time series, doesn't actually exist. There's no record of "James Riley" before his fairy tale series came out, and sources say that the man in his author photos is just an actor. It's almost as if someone made up this fictional "James Riley" identity solely to hide his true identity. But why? And who would go to such lengths? Certainly Nobody comes to mind.